Soul Cry

THIRD EDITION

OLIVIA SHAW-REEL

A Message from the Author

"Soul Cry" is where it all began—it was my very first published book, and I still can't believe how many lives it has impacted according to reviews over the years. It was written at 14 years old and released in 2015, ten years later. This is the third edition re-release with additional scenes and some character changes.

Acknowledgments

To everyone responsible for the woman I am:

My *GOD* – Father, may You be glorified with every word I write and every day that I live for You.

My *MUSE* – Baby, I appreciate you for the book covers and those fun yet intense moments of bouncing off ideas to you.

My *TRIBE* – I love and thank you for the unending encouragement. (Shaw 4, no more!)

My *SUPPORTERS* – You make writing so worthwhile!

LOVE ALWAYS,
OSR

Prologue

"Chile, we are late! Put a belt on those britches and let's GO!"

Six-year-old Jamaika perked up, as her mother's voice grew closer and louder. The yell was intended for her older brother, but she was sure that the entire neighborhood had heard her mother's strong, Caribbean diction.

The tiny bathroom that Jamaika occupied was filled with the scent of burning incense, the charred oils on the pressing comb that had straightened her kinky hair, and remnants of what was heading down the sewer with the flush.

Jamaika looked over to the door cautiously as she wiped her buttocks with two-ply toilet paper. Her mother's footsteps grew closer, paused outside of the bathroom door, and then there was silence.

"Now you've got one more time, lil' girl, to use that potty! What have I told you about going number two in your church clothes?"

Jamaika swallowed hard, hopped down from the toilet, and then flushed once more. On tiptoes, she washed her hands for 32 seconds—anything to pass the time before she was met with her mother's backhand.

The second she stepped into the living room, her arm was snatched, and she was shaken three times. "Do you hear me, lil' girl? I wan' say it no more! You undress before you poop! I paid GOOD money for that dress, you understand?"

"Yes, ma'am," Jamaika sighed.

If you asked her, these rules were stupid, but she would not dare tell her mother that. Like an obedient child, she put pep in her step and raced her brother to the family's forest green station wagon.

It was hot out and Jamaika could not understand why she had to wear stockings on a day like today. As if it was not scorching enough already outside, the car windows were sealed shut from the wintertime, so fresh air was unheard of.

They travelled in silence, other than the car backfiring two or three times. The church parking lot was packed as always, and people were literally running inside to get a good seat. Jamaika watched her white father reprimand her black mother for being late. The sight always made her giggle.

"That was your kids' fault, Nelson!" she fussed and unbuckled her seatbelt.

Jamaika held onto her mother's hand tightly as they maneuvered through the sea of moving bodies. Her brother stayed close to their father's side. She was not sure why church was so exciting and why people were in such an uproar all the time. All church was, was some sweaty guy talking loudly into a microphone, laying his hands on people's heads and making them fall backward, and then collecting money in gold baskets.

Jamaika was not impressed.

"Stop chewing that gum! Where did you even get it?" her mother commanded and Jamaika immediately swallowed the yellow substance that she had found in the backseat. "Hold your head up, child!"

Just like at home, there were way too many rules to follow in church. Jamaika had to sit cross-legged, her shoulders had to be as straight as a ruler, and her mouth was not to be opened until after service. Even her mini Bible had to sit a certain way on her lap.

She tugged at the rubber bands holding her hair together. Her lengthy, dark brown tresses were neat but too tight. Momma had pressed her hair and then gathered it into two sections with the strength of God in her fingers. Jamaika was sure that if she sneezed, her rubber bands would pop.

"I'm looking for all the young daughters in the house to come forth. All the daughters. Sister Stella, send your daughter up here too, will you?" the pastor spoke into the microphone.

Jamaika looked over at her mother who was already staring back at her with a knowing look. "Go on," her eyes seemed to say.

Jamaika would have to shimmy her chicken legs through rows and rows of strangers. The thought scared her. She clutched her mother's hand in protest, but there was no turning back. She had to obey the pastor.

Reluctantly, her mother led her up to the front of the church where other little girls stood around—some shyly kicking their feet, and others snickering behind their hands. Jamaika was by far the youngest of the bunch. She swallowed hard as the senior pastor walked over to her leisurely. His eyes were zeroed in on her like a hawk and she was sure that she would pee her pants…er, her stockings.

He held his hand out to her and when she clutched it, there was blessed oil smeared all over his palm. Actually, it was extra virgin olive oil, Momma had told her, but they blessed it after praying over it. Regardless, she didn't understand why they used the smelly substance.

The pastor smiled and the corners of his mouth crinkled like her favorite fries from the grocery store. "You're the smallest up here, sweetheart, but look all around you. All of these young girls will someday look up to you. All of these young girls will someday NEED what you have."

Jamaika blinked, not understanding.

He continued with so much power in his voice that it trembled, "Stay obedient to God, and He will always answer your prayers. Life will not be as hard, if you seek God FIRST in all that you do. If you follow His Will, He will always give you the desires of your heart. Most importantly, He will forever satisfy your soul's cry if you would just trust Him."

Jamaika did not know what any of this really meant. Life, at six, wasn't hard at all, unless you factored in learning to tell time, counting to 100 by fives, and remembering to load the dishwasher after Sunday dinner. She looked up at her mother who was now weeping with her hands lifted and then nestled her head against her mother's leg. Was her mother in pain? Why was she crying? Why was she sad?

The pastor tugged on her arm one final time. As Jamaika turned to face him, she could feel the weight of a hand against her forehead. The man created a cross on her forehead with the blessed oil, and then cupped her head.

Jamaika instantly felt warm all over and rocked in place. Her feet never left the ground, but she could feel her head tipping backward. Before she could understand what was taking place, Jamaika's eyes closed involuntarily, and she fell to the ground. It was like God Himself was cradling her now as she relaxed into the carpet. She felt weightless and light. This place, whatever it was, felt...*peaceful.*

"I've just anointed this child," the pastor continued, "so now we can all sit back and watch the Holy Spirit do wonders in her life. Of course, with great anointing comes great responsibility, and even greater distractions and hardship, but God shall be the head of her life! Mark...my...words. This child will be a mighty vessel of God! She will preach, teach, encourage, and help make the world a greater place."

"Amen!" some of the congregants shouted while Jamaika's mother joined her on the floor with tears of joy.

27 years later...

"First Lady, I have your coffee all warmed up and ready for you in your office. Your 15-minute counseling session with the Daytons was canceled after service. Your usual 4:00 dinner reservations have been made at your favorite bistro on the pier. Annnnd...do you realize you have on two different earrings?"

Jamaika had barely gotten out of her truck good, before security guards, her armor bearer, and some of the members of her church surrounded her. A good chunk of those people were excited to see and greet her, while others simply wanted to be nosey. This was the fourth or fifth Sunday that she and her husband hadn't arrived at church together, and the streets were talking.

She grabbed for her ears, plucking the teardrop earrings out one-by-one, and then studying them briefly. She sighed in exasperation, instantly regretful that she had now thrown off her entire outfit. But like most women, she knew that she had an extra, basic pair of earrings somewhere stashed deep in her purse for such a time as this.

"Blame it on my running late. I could have sworn I grabbed the red and gold ones." She rolled her eyes and tossed the earrings into the cupholder before closing the door.

"No worries at all. You know I tucked away some extras awhile ago in the front pocket of your bag."

Jamaika was never more thankful that she had packed her stilettos and worn her comfortable shoes, because dodging the rocks and grooves on the pavement while scurrying inside the church would have been a challenge. As she moved purposefully and gracefully towards the back doors of *He Lives Christian Center*, held open by one of the teenage musicians, she gave a relieved and thankful smile to her right hand woman, Akai.

"Thank you so much for always staying on top of things. Remind me to talk to Pastor about giving you a raise."

"Oh, no need. You're my girl before anything. I got you." The shorter, more petite woman gave a reassuring wink. "Speaking of Pastor…he told me you had a rough night and would be running late, so I was well aware of what I was working with this morning. Just let me know if you need anything else."

"He *told* you that?" Jamaika rolled her eyes for a second time, and prepared to stop and glare, but the security guards kept her moving to safety. "I'd hardly call last night 'rough.' I just couldn't sleep because…well, I'll tell you about it later, okay?" she added, sensing that not everyone within earshot could be trusted with the information she was ready to spill.

Her armor bearer nodded quickly, in understanding, and jotted something down in her planner. The woman was thorough, and a Godsend, and one of Jamaika's closest associates.

Jeter, the head of security, wrapped a protective arm around her back and led her inside of the expansive building. The other two guards stayed back and kept the gradually forming crowd at a safe distance. Just before the doors closed, she made sure to turn to the crowd and politely tell everyone, "God bless you all! I'm so glad you came out this morning, and looking mighty lovely in your Sunday's best. I promise we'll talk after service!"

And she meant it too. She meant every word, and like all services, promised to give everyone her undivided attention, from the first-time visitors of the church, to the long-time family friends, to the members whom she hadn't seen in months. It was what she did—it was all part of her ministry, and all part of the person she was. This morning, however, her spirit just wasn't in the mood for long, drawn-out conversations and advice-giving. She had other things on her mind and other giants to face.

The group of three moved towards the offices that were nestled on the first floor, just below the stage. In order to get to her own office, she had to pass by two other rooms—her husband's occupied office and his assistant's office. She had the smallest room, but the coziest and most furnished, in her opinion. It was feminine and smelled of potpourri and clean linen plug-in scents. Plus, it was lined, wall-to-wall, with artwork from local artists.

Jeter unlocked the door and ushered the women inside after checking to be sure everything was good to go. Only then did she give the man a pat on his massive arm, and then assured him that she was fine.

"We've got it from here. Thank you, young man." She was sure that Jeter was older than her by a few years, but the words seemed fitting with his baby face and chunky cheeks.

"My pleasure, ma'am." He bowed his head and walked back in the opposite direction. He would likely wait at the top of the stairs until she was ready to enter the side of the pulpit. There, she'd sit front and center alongside the other clergy staff.

As promised, a medium-sized mug of coffee sat on her desk with a napkin over it. Jamaika made a beeline for the now lukewarm beverage, took a generous sip, and then closed her eyes in appreciation. Akai smiled proudly, happy to have brought a sense of joy to her friend, if only for a moment.

"Thanks again, girl. Ah," she sighed, allowing the caffeine to work its magic.

"Does it need rewarming?"

"No, no. This…is just what I needed." Jamaika tapped her fingers along the cup, her nails making a clink-clink sound. "It's perfect."

"Good. So, uh, you want to talk about it now?" Akai rounded the desk and stood in front of Jamaika, who suddenly couldn't look her in the eye.

She gingerly crossed her arms under the curve of her breasts and then pressed her hip into the side of the desk.

"Later. Much later." Jamaika gave an apologetic half-smile and situated her bag in one of the chairs. Her eyes were on the plastic bag she had tucked into one of the many side pockets. It had somehow worked its way out of its hiding spot, so Jamaika stuffed it further down in the bag. "I just need to…get my thoughts together for service, if you don't mind."

Akai watched her carefully, eyeing Jamaika from her feet to the top of her head in concern. Finally, she shook her head in understanding and then pushed away from the desk. "I can only respect and accept that. Please look for me after service, or call me when you make it home. But do not let a few days pass without talking to me, okay? You know how you get."

Jamaika chuckled and nodded. "I promise I won't."

"I'll leave you be for the next few minutes. I hear the praise team getting started up there, so I'll wait with Jeter until you're ready to go up."

"Sounds good."

As Akai turned on her heel, her handkerchief skirt flowed around her body. She left with some sincere parting words, "Let whatever's bothering you roll off, so you can enjoy service and enjoy your day. See you later."

"Yeah…see you shortly."

The door closed behind Akai and all was silent except for her retreating footsteps. All was still except for the trembling in Jamaika's hands. She closed her eyes as she gathered her thoughts and attempted to calm her breathing. She knew her anxiety and panic wasn't sky-high because of the brisk walk outside, or the excitement of her rushed morning. She was aware that she was growing more and more nervous because of the decision she would soon make that she knew wasn't necessarily the answer, but it would permanently take away her physical and mental pain.

She did not bother to lock the door, but instead, grabbed her bag and headed for the private bathroom that had served as a safe place for her many early mornings and late evenings. There, she could pray, cry, and talk to God uninterrupted. It was her prayer room of sorts, and it had even been a sanctuary to Akai a time or two before. It wasn't exactly a huge space, but its earth tones gave it a warm and homey feel that was unmatched. Her private bathroom was also where she knew her life would be forever changed, in a matter of minutes.

It didn't take her long to get situated with her purse half open. She soon stood barefoot in front of the mirror, her waist pressed into the countertop, and her eyes mesmerized with the image before her. She looked flushed and unlike herself. She looked...*exhausted.*

"Just do it," the phrase fell from Jamaika's lips, covered in nude-colored lipstick. She'd pick up the cosmetic just yesterday and felt like her $11 purchase was all a waste, especially since no one had complimented her or singled her out on it. Usually, Akai was great at noticing new makeup or new hairstyles, but this morning had obviously been a blur for all of them.

Her words touched the atmosphere just above a whisper for a second time, softer but more affirmative, "Just...do it."

If there was a Nike representative nearby, she was sure that she would be compensated for her verbal advertising.

"Just do it," Jamaika muttered again, her eyes closing briefly and then reopening with a pop. This time, tears formed and her nose reddened as the emotions of the last several days, weeks, and even months seemed to weigh her down.

She took in the red A-line dress that clung to her upper body just right, and the cream and red kite scarf around her neck. With saddened eyes, she admired her half up, half down hairstyle. Her deep brown tresses were a mix of curls and straightened hair. Overall, she was the essence of what it meant to look like a First Lady. She was classy and poised—but somewhere along the line she had come undone.

Beneath her fingertips was the cool countertop; it was a dark brown and black marble that she had chosen herself. Back and forth, she rubbed the smooth surface, and became obsessed with the feel of it under her warm, cinnamon skin. Her eyes eventually left her image and locked on the orange prescription bottle that seemed to call her name. It sat next to her purse, filled with at least 23 tiny red and white pills. In fact, she knew it was 23 pills exactly because she had counted them this morning.

Color was so vivid to her right now. It seemed to hypnotize her. The joy that once ran through her veins had diminished, and the smile that normally reached her eyes, had since died. Jamaika Owens was on the edge…literally, and there was no helping her. There was no stopping her. There was no saving her. God had orchestrated her life for 33 years, and she was now taking matters into her own hands and on a Sunday morning, no less.

It was Women's Day, where she would be honored before the congregation, and celebrated by her sisters in Christ. Service was beginning shortly, as Akai had reminded her, and she was sure that someone would be rushing in soon to check in on her whereabouts. The middle-aged minister of music was in the sanctuary, singing and doing a last-minute sound check. She could hear his beautiful baritone now, creeping through the walls.

The Tasha Cobbs song that he warmed up his vocals with was her favorite worship piece, and the words caused a chill to run down her spine. Many nights, she lied awake singing the same praises and affirmations to a God she knew would be extremely disappointed in her. But at this point, she had reached an all-new low and there was just one thing left to do. She did not care about completing any other mission, but the one that was before her. It was inevitable, irreversible. She willed the beautiful worship to leave her mind.

What would Mom say? What would Dad think? Negative, impure thoughts replaced her momentary remorse and peace. Jamaika took pleasure in the idea that she could possibly be found by another member of the church. She smiled at the thought of how badly her husband would feel, upon getting the news that she had consumed these pills and succumbed to an early death. She looked forward to the afterlife—whatever it was. Surely, it was better than the hell she currently lived through.

Jamaika was a faithful member of the church, and had been a part of the ministry since it was built from the ground up. All of her earnings as a teenager and working lowly, part-time jobs went into the many building funds. Decades later, the 70,000-square foot building was the quintessence of divine growth and faithful tithe payers. She remembered moving into the building and shouting the walls down upon its re-grand opening. Praising God for hours is all she longed to do…back then.

Today, Jamaika was an unemployed married woman, mother of none, and a spiritual wreck. Years ago, she would have done absolutely anything for the church, and for the shepherd of the house. But things, much like people, changed. She barely recognized herself these days. She was tired of going through the motions. She was tired of living a lie.

Jamaika took a deep breath and muttered her favorite phrase in the last 15 minutes, "Just do it, Jay. Just…do…it."

She figured there was no better time than the present.

Leisurely, she twisted the top off of the prescription bottle. It was an old medication that she was supposed to take following the multiple miscarriages that she had suffered from. A deep depression followed, and she had been diagnosed with some hard-to-name disorder. Her husband, with the suggestions of family and friends, encouraged her to take these "happy pills" and she had not taken but a week's worth before deciding to put them away.

Until now.

Chapter One

Beep.

Why was that so loud?

Beep.

The sound grew bolder and more obnoxious.

Beep.

Okay, seriously, what was that sound?

"Oh, look, she's opening her eyes!"

"Nurse? Nurse! She's opening her eyes!"

"Jamaika, baby, can you hear me?"

"Praise God!"

Jamaika kept her eyes low, but tightened her grip around a much larger, warmer hand. It appeared to be masculine, and she knew who it was before even lifting her eyes and seeing the owner to the hand that had caused her so much distress in previous years.

"Ugh," she attempted to cough, but it came out more as an exhale.

She could feel that her body was hooked up to several tubes, and her mouth felt cottony, foamy. This was not death. This was not Heaven, hell, or any afterlife for that matter. This was a hospital room, and her head pounded as if she were a bass drum. The cadence of the beep-beeps did not help at all. Euphoria was leaving, and pain was setting in. Murmurs from surrounding people became clearer and clearer.

"Jamaika, honey, look at me!" Her mother's voice permeated the room, and it made her cringe. "It's a miracle you're alive! What...what happened to you? Why did you do this?"

Though sweet sounding and gentle with caution, Jamaika could hear the disbelief in her mother's words. Her already heavy heart dropped more, and she could not decide if she was more upset that the pills had not destroyed her life, or that her mother was by her side. As expected, the barrage of questions came in like a flood, and she couldn't keep up. She decided to keep her eyes closed.

"Sweetheart, what pushed you to…suicide, really? Have you gone mad? You…you would have gone STRAIGHT to hell if Akai hadn't found you in time and saved your life! I did not raise you this way! You're a disgrace to the Christian community!"

"Shhh! Stella, she needs rest. That discussion can wait," her father, ever the rational one, broke in, and silenced the debate. Jamaika was grateful that he had shut her mother up.

Jamaika cleared her throat despite its scratchiness and decided to finally lift her head. She faced the room that was filled with those she once considered loved ones. As of late, she had been feeling lonely, unwanted, and a downright outcast in her own skin and the black sheep in her family.

Her parents, older brother, Akai, two of the ministerial staff, and her husband, all stared back at her. A mixture of disappointment, anger, and concern filled their gazes. The intensity grew to be too much, so she closed her own for a second time and sighed.

"May I have some privacy, please?" Her throat was on fire. It felt like she had eaten a couple of hot peppers.

"Sure thing. Honey, please…when you're out and healthy and doing better, please call me,"

Akai whispered as she leaned over and kissed Jamaika's forehead. "And I mean it. I love you."

Jamaika only nodded.

"Pastor, please give her my best," one of the single, desperate women that had tagged along, whispered to her husband. Her name was Alicia…or Ayesha; Jamaika couldn't recall in her fuzzy state. All she knew was the woman was notorious at wearing blouses that fit too snugly, and skirts that weren't long enough. To be a 'minister,' she sure was skanky.

The other woman, an older minister with much more class, bowed her head towards Jamaika. She deposited a card and a few long-stemmed white roses on the way out.

Jamaika's eyes left the retreating women and then landed on her husband, Jalen. They held gazes even as her brother rubbed his hand across her forehead lovingly and whispered that he loved her. They held gazes as her mother patted her arm and walked off with tears falling from her eyes. They even held gazes as her father hugged her and told her that he was blessed that his only baby girl was still alive.

Jalen slowly loosened his tie as the door closed behind the last family member. He was the senior pastor at their church and dressed sharply in the civic attire from this morning's interrupted service. He wore a perfectly tailored and neatly steamed suit jacket, slacks, and shoes that gleamed with newness. His personalized "J-O" cufflinks even matched his ensemble. Jalen had always been a great dresser.

Jamaika stared at him as he gingerly closed the blinds and then walked back over to her. He didn't sit in one of the uncomfortable chairs or lean over her bedside. He stood erect and unmoving, as he looked her over in what she could only glean as disgust. Then, in silence, he folded his hands atop his head and began to pace. A million thoughts and emotions seemed to dance across his handsome face.

She waited for the bomb to go off. Three...two...one.

"How DARE you embarrass me like that?"

Bingo.

"How...how stupid can you be? You attempted suicide in my church—OUR church? You're the First Lady for God's sake! How does that even sound? How does that make you look?" Jalen yelled, and she knew an explicative or two would follow.

Although he was a pastor and was good at what he did, sin had crept back into his life and his lifestyle was a reflection of those shortcomings. Jalen had been pastoring for over three years and was the biggest hypocrite of them all.

He stood in the pulpit, dressed to impress every Sunday morning, Wednesday evening, and Friday night. When he was not advocating for underprivileged youth, he was preaching to lost souls, encouraging the discouraged, feeding the poor, telling husbands to remain faithful, urging churchgoers to give cheerfully, and pleading sinners to turn to righteousness and yet...

"I'll tell you how it made you look! It made you look WEAK!"

Her eyes slammed shut at the harshness of his words.

"Really, Jay? You're as dumb as they come, pulling a stunt like that. I was prepared to teach a GOOD Word and here comes Sister Akai yelling that the 'First Lady's passed out in her bathroom.' And to think...to THINK...that it was Women's Day. We had more people in attendance than usual, and you were the one being honored! So, not only did you embarrass me, embarrass your family, and ruin the service for everybody, but you embarrassed *yourself!*"

There he stood, an adulterer, two-faced friend, and liar. Like the obedient bride she was, she had put up with the foolishness. On top of that, Jalen had an unclear idea of what it truly meant to be saved and sanctified. He was an abuser when he really got upset, and the man could give any sailor a run for his money with the curse words he spewed every chance he got.

He was no angel, as everyone thought he was. He reeked of Sister Alicia...or Ayesha's perfume even now, and Jamaika wondered why her husband's alleged mistress had even come to check on her. It was probably to see if she was really dead. There was no real concern—only nosiness and pettiness as usual.

"That makes no sense, Jamaika. How...could...you...do...this...to...me?"

Jalen stopped pacing for a second and turned to look at her incredulously. His eyes darkened and she was sure that if they were not in a hospital, he would have punched the nearest wall. She swallowed the lump in her throat but then immediately regretted it since her throat seemed to hurt more.

"I hope you realize how STUPID you made me look today! Everything you do is a reflection of me—don't you realize that?"

She looked down at her hands and fidgeted. Her flesh was swollen and reddened.

22

"You're just a pitiful…pitiful excuse of a wife and First Lady," Jalen continued coldly.

Jamaika closed her eyes again, while he proceeded to go on and on about how much of a lousy wife she was. She remained still, willing the mental and physical pain to go away. Her heart ached and her stomach felt empty, probably pumped of all of its contents.

Jalen never faltered in his speech. Eventually, he stood above her and began pointing out how his church salary may lower now that members would leave. When he seemed to grow tired of hearing himself talk, he shook his head for a final and sighed.

"I just don't know what you were thinking, baby," Jalen concluded.

He rounded the hospital bed and began to gather his belongings. His Bible, his satchel, and his two phones. One was business and the other was personal, he claimed. Those were two items people always saw with him and today was no exception as he checked them both and then tucked them in his bag.

"I'm going to leave you be, and let you think about what you did to me," Jalen declared, just as a nurse peeked in to check in on her.

The woman smiled, wide-eyed, at the fact that Jamaika was up and alert. Jalen continued to talk as the woman busied herself and tried not to eavesdrop, but the task was futile.

Jalen looked away from the woman and shook his head at Jamaika like she was the scum of the earth. When he spoke again, his words slid over her like a cool towel, "I'll be back another day, or I'll send Akai and one of the other hospitality members. Don't call and disturb me, because I'll be too busy cleaning up this mess you made."

Emotionlessly, he leaned to kiss her forehead, brushed a few strands of hair from her face, and then left. As if his words weren't forceful enough, he slammed the door shut and the motion rocked the cheesy painting hanging on the wall. She was finally by herself...other than the fumbling nurse. The woman must have thought he was a monster, and she would have been absolutely right in her assumptions.

Jamaika sighed and listened absently to the woman as she gave her a rundown of what was going on, the work they had performed, and what the next few days and weeks would look like for her. Jamaika zoned in and out, unable to fully focus. If only her master plan had worked. If only the pills had made it to her stomach quicker and done the damage that she intended. If only Akai had not found her in time. If only, if only. Jamaika would be on her way to some mortuary and as far away from Jalen as she could be.

But perhaps there was more to her pitiful, sorry story. With a sad smile, she thought about her husband and the fact that not once had he asked her how she was feeling. Not once had he expressed how happy he was that she had not actually succumbed to death's call. Not once had he questioned what had caused her to take such measures.

"I'm going to grab the doctor and be back in a few minutes, okay? There are people just outside of your room, if you need anything," the nurse said, breaking Jamaika from her thoughts.

She nodded and looked at the security guards and medical personnel who stood around in the hallway in a semi-circle, probably discussing her. She was now considered unstable and would have to be evaluated, judged, and ridiculed. She was now "crazy" in everybody's eyes.

She may as well get used to it.

Chapter Two

"It's just so mind-blowing that when I came here, I was broken and feeling like the world was against me."

"And now?"

"...Now, I'm excited to rekindle my relationship with my young daughters. I'm excited to look for a new job and to reenroll in school. I'm just excited to live again!"

The room erupted into gentle applause, including Jamaika, as they congratulated the young suicide survivor. The woman did a quick up and down bounce, before she moved from the middle of the room and took her seat.

"Excellent, Tequila. We're excited for you and all that is to come for your life. Who's next?"

Life marched on, as it only could. Like all seasons, change made itself known and Jamaika morphed gracefully with it. It had been a painful few days, weeks, and even months that followed her suicide attempt, but with each day, she learned to forgive herself. She relearned that nothing was too hard for God. Everything from her unhappy marriage, to her ongoing disappointment and heartache from her miscarriages, to the unclean thoughts that often ran through her mind to end her life no longer defined her. Most importantly, she discovered how strong she really was, and that nothing or no one could break her for as long as she lived. She knew she could do anything, and she was reminded, each day, that she was wonderfully and beautifully made.

She sat now, attending her final group meeting with other suicide survivors and counselors.

It was a gathering that took place three days a week. Jamaika had shared her inner most thoughts with all of the group members and had befriended many faces. She had also made a home at the facility's rehabilitation center where she had the option to either check in daily and go home, or stay the night. To ensure she received the best treatment and attention, Jamaika opted to check-in for 30 days to the facility.

"If that is all, ladies and gentlemen, you are free to go back to your rooms. We have tacos and karaoke in the main hall tonight, and you're encouraged to come. Mrs. Owens, if you have a moment, please see me in my office."

"Sure." Jamaika stood and followed the program's director, Dr. Amelia, down the hallway. The facility was bustling with people left and right, all friendly faces, and all sorts of fun personalities. The beauty of it all was that they were there for a common reason—to receive help and healing. There were no judgments, no finger-pointing, and no ridicule.

The two reached Dr. Amelia's corner office where they both eased into chairs and stared at one another for a moment.

Jamaika was the first to break out into a shy smile. "Is...everything okay?"

"I'm just admiring how great you look. When you entered my office, you looked NOTHING like what you look now. Don't get me wrong. You were, are, and will always be beautiful. But it was in your eyes. Your smile didn't reach your eyes and your spirit didn't shine as brightly. Today, I see a woman who has been transformed. But enough about what I see. How are you feeling?"

"Thank you for those compliments. I'm feeling great and like myself again…finally. I—I have honestly never been happier," Jamaika admitted.

"That's awesome to hear. It saddens me to part ways with you, but it also warms my heart to declare that you are officially done with your treatment program."

Dr. Amelia was short and plump, with unruly, curly hair. The woman gave a toothy smile and stood, motioning for Jamaika to do the same. She leaned over the desk to regard her mentee. Her breath was warm and garlicky when she spoke, "This completes your final day of therapy, sweetheart. I am so very proud of you."

Jamaika also stood to her full height. Despite her extended hand, Dr. Amelia embraced her in a warm hug. The two had grown close over the last month and Jamaika could say she would truly miss their one-on-one and group sessions. Her faith had been restored, and her mind had been renewed. God had forgiven her, and her family and church members had obviously prayed her through because there was no way she would have made it.

Akai and Jamaika's longtime friend, Nadia, had been the perfect support system, often visiting her twice a week, and sometimes on the weekends. Her brother and parents had not been as visible; though, she understood it was because they lived over an hour away. Her parents, in particular, weren't the best highway drivers, and it was better they stayed in their neck of the woods as far as she was concerned.

Jalen, on the other hand, had only visited the facility twice. Once, he dropped off a suitcase of clothes, and the second time, he needed to ask her what seasoning to put in her special five-cheese chicken Alfredo. Apparently, he had been doing a lot more cooking in her absence, which she found absolutely ludicrous since they had a personal chef for that.

Even still, Jamaika looked forward to going back home. She did not necessarily miss her husband. She was just excited to lie in her own bed and was content to have a piece of her freedom back. The healing had been long and drawn-out and now it was time to put her faith into action.

"We will have someone drop off the rest of your belongings this week, and you're welcome to drop by our celebratory gathering this coming Saturday. It'll be a few refreshments and you're welcome to exchange information with the other patients."

Jamaika nodded and grabbed the woman's hands. "Will do, Dr. Amelia. Will do. Ah! I'm going to miss you. You gave your very best to me and the other patients, and we appreciate it. *I* appreciate it. Thank you for everything."

The women hugged for a final time and then walked out of the office, arm-in-arm.

"You take care of yourself, sweetheart. Don't hesitate to call me if you ever need anything. Remember, you've got this. Now go out and be GREAT."

Dr. Amelia waved a final goodbye and Jamaika drove away, knowing she would never look back. She had all of the resources that she needed, if ever a moment of weakness returned, but she knew that she was stronger, better, and ready for her second chance at life.

As she embarked on the lengthy drive back home, she occasionally eyed herself in the mirror

29

and smiled. Now that she was done with her rehabilitation program, there would be no more daily visits by doctors, no more monitored meals and recreation time, and thankfully, no more medications. She was free and finally looked and truly felt her best.

"Thank You, Lord," Jamaika praised softly. She decided to call her mother before anyone else.

After several rings, her heart skipped a beat. None of her family knew she was getting out of the treatment center today, but there was just something about a girl's relationship with her mother. No matter their tiffs and differences over the years, she needed to hear her mother's voice on the other end. She needed the reassurance.

"Punkin, is that you?"

Jamaika enjoyed the sound of her childhood nickname in her ear. Instantly, everything felt like new. "Hey, Momma. You busy? What are you up to?"

"I just sat down to have lunch with your grandmother. Is everything okay?"

"Everything is great actually. I'm done with my treatment and counseling, and—"

Her mother broke through her good news, "Your grandmother says hello."

"Awww." Jamaika smiled and waved as though either of them could see her. "Tell her I said hi! Where are you two having lunch?"

"There's a new restaurant here in Lindbergh that opened up, just off of the highway."

Jamaika squinted in thought, trying to envision where it was. "Oh, I know exactly what you're talking about. I heard on the news they're pretty good. I'm actually about 20 minutes away, if you don't mind me popping up."

After months of not having greasy or fatty foods, she longed for a juicy steak topped with mushrooms and onions, and a slice of strawberry cheesecake. Plus, she could catch up with the women in her life.

"That should…be okay, I guess. Come on down, baby."

They were receiving their entrees when Jamaika arrived nearly a half hour later. Her grandmother stood up to hug her, while her mother proceeded to pick over her grilled chicken and Caesar salad. Jamaika had to chuckle. Her mother was always picky when it came to non-Caribbean food, and she wasn't sure why the woman even went out to eat. Many times, as a young girl, she witnessed her father reprimanding her mother for wasting money on meals that she did not finish.

"How are you, baby?" Her grandmother—a short and feisty, dread-locked woman—cupped her face in her hands and kissed her forehead over and over again. "It's so good to see you! You've lost weight, eh? Your behind was much larger the last time I saw you."

"I, uh, guess so. I hadn't noticed," Jamaika chuckled and playfully looked over her shoulder at her backside. She then rounded the table and leaned towards her mother, holding out her arms. "No hug, Ma?"

The woman who had carried her for nine months stared back at her quietly. It was a cold, icy stare that caused the miniscule hairs on the back of her neck to stand at attention. Her mother's naturally smoky eyes held a disappointment that was similar to when she had come to visit her in the hospital.

Jamaika could see the tears that were forming, and the anxiety that was causing her cheeks to redden. She knew the lecture would come, along with the questions and the concerns. But more than anything, she wanted to tell her mother the good news. Yet, she never got the chance as she watched her mother place her fork down and sigh. The motion caused her napkin to blow across the table.

"Punkin, I've got to be honest. The time away from you allowed me to really reevaluate some things, namely where...where did your father and I go wrong?"

So much for thinking that things would go well. "Excuse me?"

"Help me to understan'." Her mother's less than stellar English became broken, as she grew frantic. "I could have lost you, and then wha'? My only girl...my only daughter! Where would that have left me and Papa? Eh? You'd be dead right now!"

"Shhh," her grandmother shushed. "This isn't the place for this discussion!"

"It must be said! She's a FOOL to have pulled what she did!"

"Do you really hear yourself right now?" Jamaika rolled her eyes. "Gosh, Momma. I wanted to tell you they released me from the treatment center today. I wanted to tell you about the friendships I made, and the things we did, and tell you about how much happier I am. I wanted to share with you about how optimistic I feel, and how much I can't wait to start my new life. I wasn't looking for judgment or a lecture. I know what I did could have hurt you all, and I've spent the last couple of months apologizing and seeking forgiveness."

Her mother wiped her mouth with the back of her hand, chuckling bitterly, "So you want a pat on your back? You want a special reward? You were released from the treatment center, okay? That's good to hear and I'm happy for you. But baby, you should have never gotten to that point! I...raised...you...better...than...that!"

"You raised me better than what? Oh, that's right. You raised me to hide my emotions and to hide behind our faith, but you didn't raise me to feel, and THAT'S the problem! Look at you, sitting there with your nose pointed and your neck stretched. You're judging me like you've been where I've been!" Jamaika's voice grew and she could see heads turning. "You preach and preach about forgiving others and not judging, and yet, you're doing the very things the Bible says not to do!"

Her mother grew quiet, and the two seemed to have a staring match. Finally, Jamaika blinked. "What?"

"Do not disrespect me."

"I'm not disrespecting you," Jamaika assured her and lowered her voice completely. She inhaled shakily and closed her eyes against the tears that threatened to fall. "Of all people, I expected to see you and Daddy. I just knew MY family would be there faithfully, helping and praying me through. But I barely saw you guys in my darkest moments, Momma. How do you think that makes me feel? What do you think that did to my confidence and my recovery?"

"You're out, aren't you? Obviously, you didn't need me when you decided you wanted to kill yourself and you didn't need me to hold your hand through your treatment."

"Oh, but I did, and that's the problem! You weren't there! You were never there—at least not in a healthy sense!"

Her mother's eyes turned to slits, as she slammed her palm down on the table and spoke through gritted teeth. "I gave you and your brother the best childhood you could ever…"

"It's NOT about my childhood or my adolescence, or what you provided for us, Momma. It's about right now! It's about the woman I am today. Look, you're sitting here with Grandma. You don't think I need you as much as you need her? You've never once just hugged me or loved on me and tried to find out why I attempted what I did. There's always the finger-pointing and the judgments, but never a desire to UNDERSTAND or LISTEN. That's what this is all about."

"Jamaika, Stella. Calm down. Calm down. Let's not be the family that gets kicked out of the restaurant. People are already looking. Let me speak." Her grandmother held up a hand and took over the conversation. She waited until both women sat down again before she grabbed each of their hands. She spoke fluidly in her native tongue for a few moments.

Jamaika was the proud daughter and granddaughter of women who had emigrated from the Dominican Republic to Louisiana, and then moved to Illinois in the latter years. Needless to say, she had grown up in a household that spoke Spanish, French Creole, and English, and it had not been easy to learn. To this day, she struggled with all of the languages from time to time.

"Could you understand what I said?"

"A little bit. What does that mean?"

The conversation halted for a second as the waitress came to take her order.

Her mother spoke up this time, her dialect a little clearer, "What your grandma said was, 'be happy with what you've got.' So many women want your husband and want what you have. Why were you so bitter in the first place? Your life is beautiful and blessed, and you have a great man who loves you."

Her grandmother, again, reached for her face and rested her palms against each cheek. She spoke slowly, "Of course we thank God you're still with us, but you have to see where WE are comin' from. How can you even THINK about sabotaging your life when you have all that good stuff going on? Eh? It's really disheartenin' that you would be so selfish, ya know?"

Jamaika chuckled in disbelief. They obviously still didn't get it, and frankly, she was tired of explaining herself. She clicked her tongue against the roof of her mouth for a few moments, thinking about her next words.

"I'll say this and then I'm done with this conversation. I am blessed for this second chance at life, yes. I thank God that He saved me, of course. I almost made a mistake that could have cost me my life. I get it. But what I needed more than anything was for my family, during this time, to tell me that it was okay and that you guys still loved me. I didn't ask for your advice on my marriage, nor do I care for your opinions. Because what you two fail to realize…"

She stood with her head high and gathered her purse and cell phone, "…is that this great man you speak so highly of only visited me TWICE

35

while I received treatment. Other than that, he has not called, sent flowers, or anything. Of course, you didn't know that because you didn't bother to come visit me either. You know what? I'm going to leave before I say something I *really* regret."

Jamaika had no desire to continue this discussion with her judgmental kinfolk who were blind to the truth anyway. All they saw was money and opportunity, and "what could be." She told the waitress she would be heading to the bar and then moved as quickly as she could away from them. It was still early in the day and the happy hour patrons had yet to pour in, so she nursed her water with lemon and looked at the sports highlights on the TV screen. She was so enthralled in her thoughts and in her subsiding anger that she did not hear the "excuse me" from the gentleman beside her until it was too late.

The same time that he sat down beside her was the same time she decided to swing both legs around and cross them. Jamaika's knee collided with the poor man's groin and he collapsed slightly into her lap.

"Oh! Oh, my God. Are you okay?"

This day could not have gotten any worse.

Chapter Three

The stranger's twisted face told her everything she needed to know. With a warm blush settling on her cheeks, Jamaika guided him to his stool and without thinking, took her glass of water and sat it on his lap. What was thought to be a helpful gesture, turned out to be Jamaika's horrible judgment.

Surprised by the coolness and her boldness, the man yelped in pain and jumped up. "Whooo! Don't...don't do that!"

Glass shattered everywhere.

"I am soooo sorry!" Jamaika explained and held her hand against her mouth in shock. She knew all eyes were pretty much on them, including those of her retreating family members, who stole a final glance her way. "I feel awful. Are you okay?"

After a moment, the stranger fell forward in laughter. His chest bounced up and down as he bellowed. A waiter walked over to help clean up the mess, and then, he spoke in a low tone, "I'm fine, but only if you promise not to do anything else."

He removed his suit jacket and hung it up behind him. Jamaika laughed this time and offered him a couple of napkins. "It was instinct, I promise. I thought the ice cubes would have helped. Please don't ask what I was thinking."

For the first time since their encounter, their eyes met and Jamaika noticed just how good looking he was. She was never one to gawk at people, especially the opposite sex, but this fella was fine and was dressed as though he had left some important business meeting. He was clean cut, neat, and smelled like fresh linen. She felt completely underdressed beside him in her simple jeans and T-shirt.

She was sure he was somebody's man, but for the moment, she appreciated God's many gifts. Besides, looking wouldn't hurt, right?

"Jamaika, correct?"

"Uh, yes." She eyed him up and down quickly in distrust, and then turned to face the bartender. She had never seen this man in her life, but she had a clue how he knew her. She threw him an unimpressed look. "Let me guess, you're a fan of my husband's?"

The stranger made a funny face. "Hardly. I've listened to your podcasts a few times and recognize your voice. You have that forum for youth pastors, right?"

"I *had* a podcast. That's correct." Jamaika could not deny that she was feeling better already. He was one of the first people to ever approach her and recognize her from her projects. "So, you're a fan of mine then?" she teased.

"You could say that. I tuned in religiously every Wednesday. A little disappointed you cancelled the show." He smiled. "But back to your question. Pastors have fans, nowadays? What happened to having just regular congregants?"

Her meal was coming now, and she could feel her mouth water at the very sight of the sizzling steak with a side of steamed asparagus that she didn't necessarily want but knew she needed to eat. She immediately shook the salt and pepper shakers over it.

"I could ask that same thing. Please excuse me while I devour this."

He lifted his hands with a hearty chuckle and seemed to understand her hunger. "Hey, I'm going to order one as well. You've got my mouth watering over here. Help yourself, Jamaika. I'm Levi."

She presumed that she had heard him incorrectly. "Um, Levi...as in the jeans that were popular in the 90s?"

"In the 90s? They're *still* popular nowadays, actually." Her new friend smirked and waved down a waiter. After placing his order, spoke again, playfully but seriously, "It's Levi, as in Leviticus."

Jamaika choked slightly and resisted the urge to laugh. A piece of mushroom flew out of her mouth and onto her shirt. She quickly brushed it off and knew for sure she had heard him incorrectly this time. "*Seriously?*"

Levi nodded and the cutest dimple appeared as he returned her smile. "I'm named after a book in the Bible. Pitiful, huh? When I was about 14, I adopted the nickname 'Levi' and it's been working for me since. Don't tell anyone I told you. Shhh."

Jamaika placed a finger against her lips, mirroring him. "Your secret's safe with me...Levi..."

They shared a soft, knowing smile and as sweet as the moment felt, she knew she could not give this man the time of day. She was still married. Plus, from the looks of his occupied left hand, he was also committed to some lucky woman. He seemed to either read her thoughts or followed where her eyes had dropped to his hand.

"Seven years this June."

Jamaika looked away in embarrassment, knowing that she had gotten caught. "Congratulations. That's awesome."

39

He shrugged nonchalantly as though it was no big deal and his expression spoke volumes. Levi motioned to her own wedding ring. "Thanks. How long for you?"

"Thirteen loooong years," she exaggerated and eyed her ring.

She remembered getting it for their ten-year vow renewal, and it was the prettiest thing she had ever laid eyes on. Adorned in chocolate diamonds, the ring was beautifully wrapped in 14-carat gold and was impressive. It sparkled genuinely even beneath the dim restaurant lighting. It was truly a beauty, and Jalen had obviously spent a lot of money on it.

However, the ring was a far cry from their love. Symbolically, she should be wearing a black ring, to reflect all of the pain, suffering, and abuse that she had endured at the hands of her husband.

"It's only looooong if everything's not how it should be," Levi pointed out and sipped on his carbonated drink from a straw.

Jamaika shrugged and looked at the television. She commented lowly, "I wonder what time the game starts tonight."

She focused on finishing her steak and decided to change the subject. Although he was incredibly sweet, her marital problems were just that—her problems. She and Levi continued their small talk, and wrapped up their meals, both with a slice of strawberry cheesecake.

A blanket of darkness had entered the sky, and like a gentleman, Levi paid for their meals and walked her to her vehicle. She could not believe how long they had been conversing like old friends. They were just a few parking spots away from one another, coincidentally. He rested his hand atop her truck. "You drive stick shift?"

Jamaika unlocked her door and threw her handbag inside. She nodded proudly, "That's *all* I've driven my entire life. I love the thrill of being in control."

Levi stared intensely at her as she talked and continued staring even after she had stopped. She questioned whether she should say something, but instead, smiled shyly back at him. Finally, he clapped his hands together and looked off into the breezy night.

"I enjoyed this. It was...refreshing to talk with someone."

She agreed and hugged herself against the breezy winds. "Very refreshing. I would say let's do it again, but that won't happen."

"Why not?"

Levi looked disappointed although he knew why. His fingers reached out to brush away a tendril of hair that had fallen in her face. For that nanosecond, she longed to have him touch more, caress more. Her eyes watered at the thought of being loved and touched, as she deserved. Her husband had not hugged her in years, it seemed.

Why these erratic thoughts were in her mind, she had no idea, but she willed them away. She looked down at her shoes, awkwardly kicking at the concrete. He seemed to spot her forming tears, and then grabbed her hand.

"Did I do something to upset you?"

Jamaika drew a deep breath and finally looked up at him. "Please don't judge me, because I know we just met, but I'm upset with myself."

Levi remained quiet while he listened. He looked genuinely concerned.

41

"I'm upset because I just met you and already I'm envisioning things."

Jamaika tried to articulate what she really wanted to say, but there was no way to really say it except bluntly.

Levi continued to rub her hand. "What are you envisioning? Talk to me."

Jamaika wiped her eyes and was sure that she sounded like a fool. "Your conversation is just so easy. It was so nice to communicate and laugh with a man without feeling like a piece of meat, or less than…oh, God!" She laughed to herself and avoided his eyes. She was sure he would run from her with this next confession. "You remind me of my husband when we first met, and I love it."

Things got quiet except for Jamaika's embarrassed sniffles. A car honked blocks away, restaurant goers walked about, a plane flew past in the distance, and yet Levi remained quiet. She immediately regretted going on her rant and knew she had repulsed him. After all, they were still strangers.

Eventually, she gathered the courage to look back up at him and began to apologize. "Listen…"

Her words were paused by his thumb pressing to her lips. "Shhh. Don't apologize and don't feel bad for sharing that."

Jamaika shook her head. The tears continued to flow. "This is so stupid. We're…I…am married."

Levi cupped her face in his hands. "It's not stupid, because from the moment I sat by you, you helped me to escape the craziness going on in my life as well."

He moved in closer and ran his thumb across her lips. "If things were different, I'd kiss you here and now," he promised.

His stare never faltered from hers. It was at that moment, Jamaika knew she had screwed up, talking to him so garishly. She had allowed him to cross the line with her confessions.

"Oh, my God. Oh, my God." She gathered herself and walked several feet away in shame.

While her marriage was certainly not perfect, she had never committed adultery or anything close to it. She thought about the trouble she would be in if her husband ever got wind of their exchange. Everything felt good, and yet nothing was right about the situation.

"You okay?"

Her thoughts consumed her so much that her knees buckled clumsily. Thankfully, Levi was close, and had caught her, or she was certain that her fall would be recorded and then posted on somebody's social media page.

"I'm good. I just have to remember a couple things, as should you."

As she steadied, Levi backed away slightly. Worry lines crinkled his perfect face immediately. "What's that?"

"I'm a woman of God first, and a wife second." Jamaika backed completely away and reached for the door handle. "As much as I enjoyed…this, it cannot happen again. I have to fix my family."

"Absolutely. I apologize if I made you feel uncomfortable," Levi said.

He kept his cool, but she could swear that she caught the frustration behind his stunning eyes.

He smiled his gorgeous smile, and held the door open for her.

"You take care, sweetheart."

The ride home was silent because Jamaika opted for no music. She simply concentrated on the road and kept the image of her husband in her mind. He had not responded to her earlier text, but she noticed she had a missed call from him. She hoped it would not be a problem when she entered their home. All she wanted was rest.

"Jalen?"

Her keys fell to the table the minute she stepped inside their home. It still smelled of new furniture and fresh woodwork, though they had been in the home for several years.

"I'm on the phone!" Jalen responded. He sounded like he was in his man cave.

She knew not to disturb him then and headed towards the kitchen to see if any major household chores awaited her. Their housekeeper, Sunni, was wonderful at what she did, although Jamaika would rather do her own dishes and everyday necessities.

Her home was clean, just as she had left it that eventful, dark Sunday morning. Their exotic fish swam happily. The windows were cleaned to perfection. Every corner was dusted and spotless. Even the white carpets looked plush and pristine. There was literally nothing more that needed to be done, so she took it as her cue to go upstairs to get ready for bed. She still could not believe what had transpired between she, her mother, and her grandmother, but she tried her best to ignore the sadness that lingered in her heart.

She rounded the corner and saw Jalen shirtless in his office, with his back turned to her.

From the waist down, he wore slacks and dress shoes. Her assumptions on his whereabouts were incorrect, but she still knew his business was his business. After all, he took care of all their corporate dealings, kept track of all of the church happenings, and had men in place to pick up any slack. She literally owned nothing and depended solely on this man. It was scary, and most importantly, it unnerved her.

One day he could decide to leave her and what would she have to her name? Literally nothing but the magenta and blue Betta fish was hers.

"Hey, man, I may have to give you a call back."

His words could be heard as she entered their bedroom. Jamaika rolled her eyes. Oh, that was a man all right. A *wo-man*! It was probably Alicia.

She tucked her assumptions away right along with the day's wardrobe, and then climbed into bed. Jalen entered the room, moments later, and she pretended to be asleep. Her back remained facing him, but she could hear the smile in his voice.

"Actually, you don't have to go so soon. She's knocked out in here."

Jamaika kept still and listened even closer. Sure enough, she heard a woman's flirtatious voice on the other end. "That's too bad she was released so soon. I miss you already."

Jalen entered the master bathroom and only closed the door halfway. "Let's set something up for next week. You can show me just how much you missed me."

"I can't wait."

Jamaika nearly choked at his next words, and felt her heart break in several million pieces.

45

"I love you." He made a kissing noise in the phone and hung up. He came back into the room, seeming to study her movements before speaking. He sat on the edge of the bed and rubbed her leg. "I forgot you were a light sleeper. How're you feeling?"

She sniffed and kept her back facing him. "Tired."

Jalen moved around, likely taking off his clothes, and settled on his side of the bed. "Well, get as much rest as you need. We have a lot of cleaning up to do in the next few weeks."

Jamaika turned completely now. "I'm not speaking with the media about this."

"You won't have to." Jalen paused to yawn obnoxiously. "I've hired a family spokeswoman and she'll take care of everything. I just need you to take some photos with me and attend a couple press conferences, and we're good to go. She said this should all blow over in a few weeks."

Jamaika shook her head and turned back to face the window. "Spokeswoman? Oh. Is that who you were saying 'I love you' to?"

"Of all the things I just said, that's ALL you're focused on? Don't start tripping now."

"I'm not doing anything," Jamaika affirmed. She grew quiet and then turned to peer over her petite shoulder. "Did you miss me even once while I was away?"

Her question went unanswered, and she imagined he was pretending to be asleep. She turned back around and stared at the shadows on her wall until sleep embraced her.

Chapter Four

"At this time, while the spirit of God dwells, I want to open up the doors of the church," Jalen said into the microphone that he always used on Sunday mornings.

It was red and black and contained a label with his name scrawled across it. He stood in his civic wardrobe with a hand tucked in his pants pocket. He was no longer just a regular family man, but he was now Senior Pastor Jalen. He spoke to the plentiful visitors who had stopped in for their eight o'clock service.

"In these perilous times, you first NEED a Savior, and then you need a house of worship. You need people who can cover you and pray you through."

"Amen," Jamaika spoke, dressed in her traditional First Lady attire.

This was her first time back in the church since her incident and she felt off. All eyes seemed to be on her throughout every part of the service, analyzing her and judging her. Some showed empathy and understanding, while others were unmoving and emotionless. She had even heard and caught many members, at some point, whispering about her. From her weight loss, to the paleness of her skin, to the way she wore her hair—everything was scrutinized and dissected, and she hated every minute of the experience.

It was too soon, in her opinion. She should have dragged out her "vacation" a little longer, because the forced smiles and false concern was becoming too much for her.

She was seated in the pulpit, in her usual place, at the center of other elders and deacons. Her legs were crossed at the ankle, and although she wore a slip underneath her skirt that reached mid-calf, she still draped a scarf atop her knees. Following worship, she had removed her tall heels, and replaced them with comfortable sandals.

Jalen wiped the sheen of sweat from his face with a towel. "Even if you just want to be placed under watch care, we would still love to have you. Is there anyone here today? Come now."

Several people walked up, and Jalen motioned to his ministerial staff.

"Hallelujah," he spoke lowly.

He recited a general prayer over the individuals joining and got their names. One of them was a returning visitor that Jamaika immediately did not care for. She noticed the way Jalen hugged the woman so snugly that Jamaika didn't know where she began and where Jalen ended. Her name was Malia, Jamaika remembered. The woman touched his face, as if they were old friends, and chuckled in a cutesy way.

Jamaika followed the woman with her eyes until she sat down. They seemed to catch eyes, and then Malia looked down to her young son uncomfortably. Jamaika was so sick of these women popping up out of nowhere and throwing themselves at her husband. Moreover, she was tired of her husband entertaining it.

Her thoughts were interrupted as Jalen prepared for dismissal. "Before we leave, I just want to say this."

He looked over lovingly. Like the actor he was, he walked over and extended his hand to Jamaika. She stood beside him and he tucked her against his side, kissing her forehead. The women in the congregation, fascinated with the integral man that he portrayed to be, seemed to all turn to their spouses and scowled.

"This is my wife's first time back at the ministry, in a few months. Some of you may know why, and some of you may not know, but I just want to tell her how much I love her, and I'm thankful that God healed her body, and renewed her mind," Jalen said.

He walked over to the musician's corner. The organist began playing a jazzy rendition of "You Are So Beautiful," and Jalen began to sing.

Jamaika's cheeks warmed with a blush. She could not decipher if it was from anger or from humiliation. He had always had a decent voice, but it was the gesture that boiled her blood. Just days before, he had told some woman on the phone that he loved her, and now he was attempting to be the sweetest man alive in front of spectators. This man deserved an Oscar.

"I've prayed many sunrises and sunsets for you, and God answered my prayers. To our church family, we thank you. To those who stayed, we appreciate your support. First Lady looks good, doesn't she?" Jalen added with a smirk. "Keep her lifted up."

"Yes, she does!" One of the mothers stood up, waving her handkerchief.

"Thank you so much. God bless you all," Jamaika spoke into his microphone. She hugged her husband for show, and then blew a kiss to the congregation. Her hands shook so intensely with her anger that she tucked them at her sides and grasped at her skirt.

49

As church let out shortly after, and the maintenance crew prepared the sanctuary for a second service with the associate pastor, Jamaika became surrounded by all of her spiritual children. Most of them were elated to see her back and looking better than ever. She gave out hugs, accepted gifts, took pictures, and even held newborn babies that had entered the world while she was away.

"You ready to go, Jay?"

She looked up from a young boy who had drawn a Get Well card. Jalen was looking on with impatience and a tight-lipped smile. He wasn't a small guy by any means, but he looked tiny compared to his neighboring security team, donning all black from head to toe. Jalen was normally cranky after service until he ate dinner, and today was no exception.

"I'm coming," she said and then kissed the boy's forehead and tucked his card in her purse. As much as she loved her members, the added attention didn't make her feel good. She absolutely hated it, in fact.

She knew there were consequences to all things under the sun. Unfortunately for her, she had placed her church and its members in a rocky situation. Because Jalen was a televangelist and well-known pastor, his reputation had been stained from her suicide stint. Not only that, but a few sponsors of the ministry had also backed out because they figured she was too unstable to receive their donations and go forth with any future projects or ministerial opportunities.

Yet and still, she would keep her head high and move forward in faith. It was all she could do. It was all she had to cling onto.

50

Despite the anxiety and dread to face another day of judgment and mockery, morning rolled around. It was time to hit the ground running, whether she was ready or not. With the warm, rising sun came the realization that life was forever changed for Jamaika, Jalen, their church and their brand.

To combat any rumors or further speculation, Jalen's proclaimed "spokeswoman" put together a series of press conferences filled with all kinds of big-named media outlets, journalists, and organizations. Jamaika was dolled up with a French twist, in her fitted black jumpsuit and bold red lipstick. She had been given clear instructions to just smile and keep her mouth closed, while Shay, the spokeswoman, did all of the talking.

"Jamaika, which treatment center were you admitted to?"

"No comment, thank you."

"Jamaika! Over here. What pills did you consume?"

"No comment, thank you."

"Jamaika, you look great. What kind of treatment did you receive?"

"No comment, thank you."

Like a puppet, she smiled her biggest smile and waved at all of the flashing cameras. She was grateful she had on dark sunglasses, because the flashes were blinding. The paparazzi section was thick as she and Jalen completed their fourth and final press conference for the day. They were attempting to win back the hearts of churchgoers, city officials, and other sponsors.

Their church was the biggest in Arlington Heights, and one of the largest in the Midwest with over 10,000 members, two award-winning mass choirs, and a progressive praise dance ministry. As a result, Jalen and Jamaika were afforded once in a lifetime opportunities to travel for free, host marriage conferences, and much more.

Shay had done an excellent job of contacting reporters and several local news outlets. People had shown up by the numbers to see how well Jamaika looked and ask her whatever came to mind. Thankfully, after this week, she could go back to hiding. Her face and story was featured in every publication she could think of, along with hurtful headlines and allegations. She hated anything that put her on the forefront, but she knew it was all her fault. She vowed never to compromise her Christianity and family ever again.

"Jamaika, what pushed you to this point? Can you at least answer one question?"

"No comment, thank you."

The persistent male reporter who was closest to her shoved his microphone in her face while he questioned, "What's the point of a press conference if you're not going to say anything?"

"Sir, back up!" Jeter growled. "All of you in the first row, please give them some room."

No one really budged as they murmured amongst themselves.

"Back up NOW, otherwise we'll shut this press conference down!" Jeter reiterated.

Their security team was top-of-the-line and not to mention intimidating to the eyes, so the media personnel all took a collective step back. The distance, however, did not stop the invasive and insensitive questions.

A young woman stepped forward then and raised her hand. Jamaika had not answered any questions as instructed, but she was able to call on people and say, "No comment," whenever Shay felt it was okay. She prepared to do the same with this young lady.

"First Lady Owens, I have nothing but respect for you. I was a fan of your podcast; I have followed you and your husband on social media. I attended a few services and conferences where you've spoken, and like I said, I just have the upmost respect for you."

Jamaika bowed her head in thanks, smiling.

"I say all that to say, I have been there before. I have been EXACTLY where you were and where you are now. I was prepared to end my life a couple years ago, following a messy divorce and custody battle over my children. I understand your thought process. I understand being at the lowest of lows. I...almost pulled the trigger," the woman explained, her hands shaky as she held a recorder and microphone. "But thankfully, like you, I was saved in time. Is there any advice you would give to someone struggling with suicide?"

Jamaika was taken aback. She did not expect such a confession from someone, nor did she expect the empathy and show of support. She appreciated it all the same as she took a deep breath and nodded. "Absolutely. Great question."

The woman's words tugged on her heartstrings, and she knew she could possibly save a life if she was transparent and spoke from the heart. She thought of the best answer to give the woman, while leaning forward to cup the base of her microphone.

"What are you doing?" Both Shay and Jalen leaned over and questioned simultaneously. Jalen had his hand around her back and had tightened his grip on her in warning. "Jay. Keep your mouth closed."

She held up a hand to cut him off. "You know, it's disheartening because the first thing people say about someone who committed suicide is that they were selfish. That they were thinking of only themselves, and that they could have or should have found help. But coming from a woman who 'has it all' and still attempted to end my life—that couldn't be further from the truth. Wanting to remove yourself from a toxic situation is not selfish. If anything, it's selfless. People who have committed suicide have exhausted all options; they've looked for help in all the wrong places. They've searched for someone to understand and empathize with them, and they come up short each time."

Cameras flashed. Reporters scribbled in their notepads, and Jamaika closed her eyes, going back to that infamous day.

"I know for me," she continued, despite Jalen and Shay both hissing in her ears, "It was my final option. I had had enough, and I thought it was best if I left the earth. I figured I would be doing the people around me a favor. But that's not true. So, to whoever is listening now, or to whomever will see this interview days, weeks, or even months from now, my prayer is that you realize you are MORE than enough. It may seem hopeless, helpless, and lonely. It may feel dark, and you may think your life doesn't matter but it does. I would also say to think of your perfect and loving Father. He made you for a reason, and gave you a life of passion and purpose. Suicide takes all of that away. Suicide robs you of the joy that comes after the storm."

Jamaika had all eyes on her as she spoke her truth. She gave a half-smile that eventually evolved into a small chuckle. "Naturally, I'm inclined to speak from a spiritual perspective, so hear me out, guys. If He made and created you, then He can bring you out of whatever situation that you deem too hard! Know that nothing is too hard for Him, and even when you feel like you have nowhere to go or nowhere to turn, know that He's ALWAYS with you."

Many of the reporters continued to scribble as she paused to wipe the tears from her eyes. Some had stopped writing and were hanging onto her every word. The woman who had asked the question was nodding with tears in her own eyes.

"I know it's easier said than done," Jamaika added. "Even if you do not have a support group or family who understands your pain, you have to love yourself enough to think positive thoughts, get help, look depression in the face and say…"

Shay stood up abruptly, and pulled Jamaika away from the crowd and away from the microphone. Jamaika stumbled into Jeter, who steadied her quickly, and then placed his hands back at their rightful place.

"What are you doing? I wasn't finished!" Jamaika shouted.

"You're DONE!" Shay hissed. She turned back to the crowd and her high-pitched voice crackled with panic. "Thank you, everyone, for all of your questions and for coming out today. At this time, Pastor and First Lady Owens must leave for another engagement, so this concludes our press conference. Thank you!"

To a generous amount of booing and verbal dismay, Jamaika was whisked away by a member of security. She knew that she should have kept quiet but saving a life was more important than saving face as a First Lady. She ducked her head and ran, hand in hand, with Jalen, to a limousine truck waiting in the back of the building.

Shay climbed into the passenger seat, and the moment all doors closed, the driver sped away. Jalen was silent, grinding his teeth together intently. She could hear it from where she sat. She imagined he had a mouthful for her but kept silent as well.

Their truck rode several blocks down, and Jamaika noticed the stares from other cars, cyclists, and pedestrians. People were naturally wondering who was riding in such a prestigious, commanding vehicle. "If we're trying to keep a low profile, why are we riding in a big limousine truck?"

Jalen looked from the window, to where she sat. There was exasperation all over his face. Shay looked back and rolled her eyes.

"Like MOST of my celebrity clients, I booked you guys this vehicle because it's roomy and has tinted windows."

"We're not celebrities, for one," Jamaika challenged, "Two, we're in Arlington Heights, Illinois. It's not like we're in New York or Los Angeles where people see these things regularly. The bigger the vehicle is, the more attention you'll receive. That's just common sense and contradicts what we're trying to do here."

"Oh, you're one to talk with all that babbling you did back there! We specifically agreed that all you had to say was 'no comment!' Not only did you speak and say too much, but you made me out to be the bad guy!" Jalen spoke up now, and Shay seemed to smile because he was defending her. "You should appreciate all the things that Shay has done and continues to do to clean up YOUR mess."

"Thank you, Pastor. It's nice to know my hard work is not in vain."

Jamaika scoffed. "Hard work? What, bending over for my husband while I was away?"

Shay sat in shock.

Jalen was just about ready to explode beside her. He pushed away from the seat and rolled up the partition. "Give us a minute."

Just as soon as they were hidden from view, he took the back of his hand and with incredible might, smacked the side of her mouth. The pop was so pronounced that she thought her jaw was broken. She could taste the coppery flavor of blood on her tongue.

"You better hope and pray that this little stunt you pulled for a SECOND time doesn't hurt anything else attached to my name. Jamaika, I swear to God, you better hope and pray that this all blows over. Otherwise, I'm all over you like white on rice and the only way you'll get away from me is if I kill you myself. You understand me?"

The iciness of his words was enough to send a chill down her spine. Jalen had a knack for saying many things and he tossed around threats on a regular, but this one scared her. This one came with a promise. Jamaika kept quiet and nursed her injured face until they arrived at their gated community a half-hour later. Shay stayed inside as the Hispanic driver walked around to open the doors. His eyes widened slightly at Jamaika's disheveled image. He, of course, looked away in fear as Jalen eyed him, daring him to say or do anything.

Shay seemed to chuckle in amusement, seeing Jamaika's meeker and much quieter demeanor. "Have a great day, you two," she called out sweetly.

"I'll give you a call later. Thanks again for everything you did," Jalen told Shay. "And I mean it. I owe you."

When he leaned in to kiss her cheek, Jamaika noticed how his lips lightly grazed the corner of her mouth instead. Shay shooed him away, giggling like a schoolgirl. Jamaika turned her back on their exchange and pressed her hand to her swelling jawline. Hurriedly, she entered their home and ran to the upstairs master bathroom to survey the damage he had done.

She rubbed her fingertips along her skin and winced at the pain. Her self-reflection ended quickly as, moments later, Jalen appeared in the room and looked upset all over again.

"Are you happy with what you've done? Do you see how all of this affects everybody? You should be on your knees thanking Shay for even taking on this cleanup job. We're high-profiled people, and now the focus is on the wrong things."

"I'm not going to keep apologizing," Jamaika declared. "And get over yourself. We're not high-profiled people. We're a part of a high-profiled ministry, yes—but we're regular people who make regular mistakes. Why can't you get that? Celebrities kill themselves all the time or attempt to kill themselves. I know we're held to a higher standard being at the forefront of a church, but nobody's perfect, Jay. You, of all people, should know that."

She placed her hand on his chest and gently pushed past him to leave out of the bathroom. Her eyes were on a lightweight nightgown, peeking out from the other lingerie pieces in her walk-in closet. She needed relief from her clothing and invasive undergarments. On her way over, she couldn't pull the bobby pins fast enough from her hair, allowing her tresses to fall wildly around her face. It felt good to be free.

Jalen followed behind her, so closely that she could feel the warmth of his breath on the back of her neck.

"I did my wrong, and I admitted to it. Move on."

Jalen grabbed her arm and swung her around. "But see, that's where the problem comes in." He motioned around the room with his hands. "This empire I've built so strategically and purposely, has fallen apart because of that little stunt you pulled. You think they'll let me run for mayor with this stuff on my records?"

"On YOUR records? AH! How selfish." Jamaika yanked her arm from his grip. She rubbed at the spot where his nails had dug into her skin. "My life, my confidence, and my reputation has suffered, too, you know."

"How so?"

She stood and looked him eye to eye. It was at some point that she loved when they had their cute little staring contests. Lately, he had become so evil, so menacing.

"Well, for one, look at what you do to me! Each time you put your hands on me, or humiliate me in front of people, a part of me dies. Don't think I didn't notice your flirting with Shay just now, either. You speak on integrity and all these different things while you're in the pulpit, but the MINUTE you come down, you're living a lie, Jalen."

59

His eyes widened, so she continued.

"Does your beloved church know about your affairs? Do they know we hardly lay in the same bed anymore? Do they know that you didn't check on me while I was away? Do they know you beat on me like I'm a freakin' Everlast punching bag? Let's not just dwell on my sins and mistakes because you have plenty to go around."

A smirk tugged at Jalen's full lips. The smirk turned into a full-fledged smile. Then he began chuckling uncontrollably, and for a while she saw another side to him. He was truly delusional and had lost his mind.

"Who pays the bills around here? Huh?" he stopped laughing abruptly and asked.

Here we go, she thought. "You do."

"Who takes care of all the finances and makes sure we're good from all angles?"

"You do."

"Who schedules all of our..."

She cut him off and became irritated by his cockiness. "*You,* Jalen. You do. What's your point?"

"What's my point?" Jalen questioned. He smugly threw his hands up and walked away. He headed to his own walk-in closet and pulled off his shirt. "My money, my home...my rules. I can say whatever I want to say in my house. I don't owe you an explanation, and the only person I answer to is GOD!"

"Yeah, okay, Jalen."

For a while, he dressed in silence. "Oh, and we're going out to eat at that new restaurant on Milwaukee Avenue."

"I don't feel like going out to eat. Can we just pick up some food?"

He popped his head back into the room. "I was talking about Shay and me, but I can bring something back for you, if you'd like."

Jamaika's heart dropped. She shook her head and headed down to the living room. This was not even worth arguing or fighting for anymore. "It's fine. I'll figure something out. Do you."

Alone, and in for the night, she ordered a pizza and watched back-to-back movies until the movies watched her. Their personal chef and housekeeping staff were off for the next few days, and she was happy for the "me time." She remained curled up on the couch, even after Jalen stumbled in just after three in the morning, reeking of alcohol, cigarette smoke, and God only knew what else.

"Baby? Come lay with me."

Jamaika ignored his slurs and furrowed deeper in her blanket.

"Bae! Baaaae. You hear me, girl?" His voice grew closer and more demanding, and she feared that he would do something crazy.

"Yes, Jalen?" She peeked beyond the fleece blanket. His eyes were as red as her nail polish.

"Come lay with me," he repeated.

He was extending his hand for her to grab, and reluctantly she took it. Her nightgown slid up in the process and he roughly smacked her buttocks. She led him up the stairs, and he could not seem to keep his hands to himself.

"Quit it, Jalen." Jamaika adjusted her gown, only to have him pull it upwards on her body again. "Don't do that. Please stop!"

"Why can't I touch you?" he yelled and yanked on her gown once more. This time, the thin material ripped between his fingers. "You're my wife!"

Now he wanted to throw around the title for his benefit. Just hours earlier, he had talked down on her like she was nothing. Now he couldn't seem to get enough of her. Jamaika stood, frozen in place, as he pinned her against the door. His lips ran up and down the length of her collarbone, and the tartness of his breath made her gag.

"Stop it, Jalen! You're DRUNK and you— you stink, too!"

His movements became more and more aggressive as he pulled on her, and she pushed back on him. They ended up tussling and falling to the floor. Jalen wrapped his large hands around her neck, and held her down while he straddled. With every word, his hold grew tighter and tighter.

"What's wrong with you? Why won't you lay with me? Why won't you make love to me?"

Jamaika attempted to pry his hands from her neck. "I can't breathe. Pl—Please stop."

Against her will, Jalen forced himself on her right then and there. As she cried, he professed his love, and as she pushed him away, he held on tighter. When he finished, he crawled away from her, and collapsed near the side of his bed. His snores rang out unattractively, and after about an hour, she was finally able to move her lower half.

Clumsily, she moved through the darkness and tiptoed over strewn clothes to the bathroom. The floor felt cool beneath her feet as she scurried and made it to the toilet just in time. Jamaika grew sick and emptied the contents of her stomach. She took a towel and wiped her mouth.

"Ouch!"

How silly of her to forget the raw skin on her face. The cuts and wounds seemed to burn all the more as she dabbed a towel over her cheeks. She took a quick shower, as hot as her body allowed, and then with a towel draped around her shoulders, she examined herself more. Her body ached and was a blue-black shade where Jalen's punches had cruelly landed. She felt ugly, and her smile looked distorted...fake.

"What am I doing to myself?" she spoke softly, leaning in so closely that she saw the emptiness in her eyes, the ache in her heart, and what scared her most, the defeat that was written all over. The last time she appeared this distraught and broken was right before she took all those pills. Had she hit rock bottom again, so soon?

"Sweetheart."

Another voice entered her personal meditation and thoughts, and her body jerked forward. She ended up slamming her head into the mirror. Jalen was in the doorway, staring back at her through the reflection.

"You scared me," she sighed.

He stepped forward and pulled her back against him by her hips. His hands fisted in her hair and pulled until her neck could stretch no further.

"I love you, baby," Jalen whispered and leaned in to kiss her softly. "Come back to bed with me. I want to show you just how much I love you, and how sorry I am."

He had somehow sobered up and was giving her a sincere look. She had heard his words before, heard this explanation before, and yet she believed him this time. "You really hurt me tonight, Jalen. Your words and your actions. They cut me deep."

"Shhh, that was all that liquor. You know I would never hurt you intentionally."

Jamaika began to speak but he touched his fingers to her lips, silencing her. Jalen's bloodshot eyes pierced into hers still and began to water with his words.

"You're my wife and my life. I need you. Nobody, and I mean *nobody,* can love me like you can."

Tears sprang to her eyes simultaneously, and her body cried one thing while her voice said another. "When you hurt me, I feel like I'm nothing, baby. You and I both know that I deserve better."

Her limp body gave into his, and he picked her up, sitting her on the countertop. He nestled his face in her chest, hugging her with a gentleness that she had never experienced from him.

She was not sure what had changed between being sloppy drunk, raping her, and then sobering up, but she hoped that he was sincere in what he said.

"I'll show and give you better, I promise," Jalen vowed and cupped her backside. He walked with her back into the bedroom. He gently placed her on his side of the bed and kissed her slowly with passion. "Just don't leave me. Please don't leave me, baby."

Jamaika closed her eyes as he wiped her tears. He was the gentlest he had ever been, and she was so exhausted.

"No more, Jalen. No more liquor. No more women. No more lies, and please…no more abuse."

"No more," Jalen repeated and climbed into bed beside her. Securely, he held her in his arms. He seemed afraid to let her go, and just before succumbing to sleep, he whispered, "I swear."

Chapter Five

Meet me at the house for lunch.

Jamaika looked down at the text message as it came through, later the next morning. Her mother had been missing in action since their blowup at the restaurant, so she was surprised to receive the message. It was almost like her mother felt her spirit. The drive would take a good amount of time, but she needed to get away and looked forward to the scenery and the peace and quiet.

Peeling herself from the bed, and informing Jalen of her plans, she sent a simple reply back, agreeing to go. Then she prepared for the day, with a sigh, and showered. Just before heading out, she caked on a good amount of moisturizer, concealer, and powder foundation. Her scrapes could still be seen through the makeup, but the blue and purple bruises were not as nearly noticeable.

"Be safe, baby," Jalen called out.

The rich aromas of authentic Caribbean cuisine could be smelled as soon as Jamaika stepped from her vehicle more than an hour later. She smiled to herself and entered the back of the house with her spare key.

"Ma? I'm here."

"Come on in, Punkin. Glad you could make it."

Jamaika erupted in giggles. Her mother was facing the stove and was dancing to some old school music. She was dressed in a knee-length dress that had an intricate red, white, and blue pattern. Her mother's hips swayed rhythmically, while her singing voice attempted high, off-key notes. She even shimmied her shoulders to the beat as though she had not a care in the world.

Jamaika looked around. Her father was probably off somewhere hunting up north or away with his golf buddies, doing typical white guy things. The image of her dancing, carefree mother reminded her of her childhood, minus her older brother running around and getting into mischief. Her childhood home was still well kept, and had been remodeled over the last decade.

This was home.

Despite whatever tiffs and fallouts, they had endured, she was always a momma's girl and was excited to be in her mother's presence. Just to hear her voice again was a breath of fresh air.

"You're still the same ol' jazzy Stella," Jamaika said with a hint of playfulness in her tone.

Her mother continued to dance and stir her concoction of gumbo, and then chuckled. "That's right! Ya betta know it! How's my Punkin doing?"

"Alright, Momma," she answered honestly and leaned against the doorframe. "I'm alright."

Her mother finally whipped completely around and danced over to stand before her youngest child.

"Just alright? Surely, you're more than all right. Baby, the sun is shining, God is good, and…" her mother's words faded, and she gasped, "What happened to your face?"

Jamaika swallowed hard and attempted to duck her head from view. Her mother's hand brought it back up with gentleness.

"Did he do this to you?"

Ashamedly, Jamaika nodded. "Yes. It's not the first time, Ma."

Her mother's face dropped, and she walked over to the CD player to stop the music. "What? Why didn't you tell me, love?"

"I've tried, but you guys always defend him. Jalen is a monster. He's done it all."

"Done it all like *what*? This—" she pointed to Jamaika's face. "This is ENOUGH! Punkin, talk to me. Sit. Sit." She tugged on her daughter's arm so that they were seated across from one another. "I can't believe this!"

Jamaika sighed and knew that she had to tell everything or nothing at all. Perhaps there was a reason that her mother reached out to her out of the blue. It was probably God's way of finally mending their relationship and drawing them closer.

"When did this start?"

"Well, we've been married for 13 years and together for 15, so I would say seven years now. The cheating started about four years ago," Jamaika added softly. "You, Dad, and Grandma thought so highly of him that whatever I said went in one ear and out the other. This is what I was trying to tell you at the restaurant. This is nothing new, Momma. It's not right, but it's nothing new."

Her mother looked hurt. She shook her head in disbelief and then placed her hand to her bosom.

"Honey, have I been that far out of the loop that you could not come to me? I know I may get a little emotional sometimes and I can be a little stubborn. But has it really gotten that bad that your own mother failed to see the signs?"

Jamaika nodded and began to speak.

"Oh, Punkin!" Her mother cried out. "I have done the very thing I promised that I would never do to you! I have failed you as a mother.

You've been hurting all of these years and I ignored you."

"Shhh. No, no, don't say that. You've been a great mother. It's just that…"

"There is no excuse, Jamaika. I know we preached that divorce is out of the question and that you should always fight for your marriage, but I never realized it was this bad. You've been going through this all of these years and you could not even come to me. I feel awful, and I am so sorry, baby. Please forgive me," she pleaded with tears brimming her almond-shaped eyes.

"Momma, it's okay. Really."

"It's not!" Veins popped in her mother's neck. "No wonder you wanted to take your own life. You had no one to turn to!" Her mother broke down and buried her face in the palms of her hands. "What hurts most is that my mother did me the same way, and I vowed that I'd be different. Your grandma knew that your father beat me every day of our marriage and yet she told me to suck it up. She told me to stay and fight back and pray, but divorce wasn't an option, so I had to figure it out."

"Wait, wait! Daddy HITS *you*?" Jamaika questioned in anguish. She could literally see the movie reel of her childhood flashing in her mind, thinking back to any red flags or signs.

"He *used* to hit me," her mother corrected and pressed her index finger into her temple. "It's what his father did to his mother, and it was a curse that I knew I had to break. I got wise and beat him at his own game before he killed me. I boiled a pot of hot water one night and threw it on him in his sleep."

Jamaika felt the world tilting with this new information. "I don't remember any of that."

"Oh, you were young. You wouldn't have recalled any of that."

"So, what happened when you poured the water on him?"

"I'm still with him, right?" Her mother looked at her smugly for a moment. "He has never laid a finger on me ever again, and let's just say…your father doesn't wear shorts for a reason, Jamaika."

This was literally the first time that she had heard any of this kind of talk. It saddened her that they each had so many dark secrets, but she was forever grateful that they were breaking those chains now.

Her mother walked up to the stove and decreased the heat under one of the gigantic black pots. If memory served Jamaika correctly, that was her stew/gumbo pot. "I'll be the first to apologize for my behavior at the restaurant. I did not handle the situation like a mother or like a Christian. I judged you, I blamed you, and I didn't offer any support when you needed me most. I cannot apologize enough for my ignorance. It has kept me up all night since that day. That's the reason I called you over today, baby."

"What matters most is that you recognized it. I don't hate you and never will. We both said some things we regret that day."

"So where does this leave you two? Are you still with him?"

"I am…for now," Jamaika admitted and exhaled. "For some reason, I just cannot leave him alone. Plus, he's promised that he won't do it anymore."

"Oh, honey, they always promise that."

"But I truly believe him. There was just something in his eyes."

Her mother nodded slowly with pursed lips. "Do you want me to get Papa involved?"

"No, definitely not. I don't want to upset Daddy. I just need your prayers. If it's meant to be, then I know God will turn this all around. But if he's not meant to be my husband, then God will give me the opportunity and strength to move forward."

"It is so. I cannot tell you what to do. You know that you deserve better, and if nothing else, I have always taught you that, growing up."

"I hear you, Momma."

"Now, you be careful, baby, and please call me anytime you'd like, okay? Don't you stand for the ignorance anymore, you hear?"

"Yes, ma'am," Jamaika whispered as they embraced for the first time in years. She felt the weight of the world leave her shoulders as her mother rocked her back and forth. It was amazing that, since she was a child, her mother always had a distinctive sweet scent that lingered. She would always remember it and think of the good old days of getting her hair combed, while seated in her mother's lap. That scent represented peace and comfort, and gave her indescribable strength.

When she made it back home, several hours later, she was still full with laughter, love, and good food. She headed up to the bedroom with a sigh. The lights were off and when she moved to turn them on, they miraculously popped on. It was Jalen's doing. She was briefly startled as she took in his bare chest, where he coolly leaned against the wall nearest to the light switch.

"Where have you been all this time? Who were you with?" He was already full of questions and she had not even taken her shoes off.

"I was over my mother's, remember? We spent the day, talked, laughed, and watched a movie. Don't start."

"I'm not," he assured, holding up his hands. "I was just wondering if you'd stopped off somewhere else. Jeter was wondering if he should accompany you, but I told him you were in familiar territory. Hey. Let me get that for you."

His voice was different. He sounded almost hoarse, as if he had been crying. His complexion was a little on the pale side, and he looked repentant.

"What's wrong?"

"Nothing." He helped her out of her shoes one by one, and then began to ease her arms out of her shirt. "Get comfortable. I haven't massaged you in ages."

"I've noticed," she joked, allowing him to take over. "What's gotten into you?"

Instead of answering, he fell to his knees before her and nestled his head against her stomach. His shoulders shook as he burst into tears and gave what she called an "ugly cry." Jamaika was truly thrown off by this and had no idea what to do other than rub his back.

"Why are you crying, baby?"

He was quiet for a long moment as he composed himself. "I, uh, I thought you were out cheating or had left me for good."

"And that would make you sad?"

"That would kill me."

Her hands paused slightly against his back. "So, when I tried to take my life, did that make you

71

sad too? Were you this upset then and just didn't show it? What—what happened to us, baby?"

"I don't even know myself anymore," Jalen confessed and stood up slowly. "I'm just a mess. I need to get back right with God and with you. Otherwise, I'll be on the road to self-destruction."

"You already are by putting your hands on me and by leading the double life you've grown so comfortable with. Let's just start all over. Let's make it like it was."

"Would you like that?" He peered down at her and continued to hold his arms around her frame.

"I would love it," Jamaika responded simply. "It would be an answered prayer. I did not marry you to divorce you. When I signed up for this, I agreed to the good and bad. We've had quite a few rough patches, but if you're in, baby…I'm in."

"C'mere, Jamaika," Jalen instructed gently.

They leaned into one another for a moment, swaying and eyeing each other tenderly. For the first time in a long time, there was no malicious intent behind his words. There was no anger or frustration backing up his touches. There was no disrespect or degrading comments coming from his words. He only wanted to show her what she meant to him and Jamaika loved every minute.

Jalen bent forward and nuzzled his nose against hers before kissing her forehead, each cheekbone, and then her awaiting lips. His movements were delicate and unrushed. He bent at the knees to pick her up from the floor, held her in his arms for a moment, and then placed her down on the bed. She stretched out against the plush bedspread and sighed into his mouth. Gradually, he eased a leg between hers and relaxed all of his weight into her body.

It felt good to be held by him, loved by him. Whether this was day one of a new beginning, or another "good" day in their chaotic marriage, she gave her concerns to God and gave her body to Jalen as if it was their first time all over again.

Chapter Six

"Oh! This feels so, so good."

Beads of water slapped against Jamaika's backside as she leaned to shave the few hairs on her legs. She had to be flawless today, or close to it. Today was family photo today, and she was excited to showcase the brand-new outfit and shoes that Akai had picked up for her from her favorite boutique.

Jalen was on the outside of the shower door, brushing his teeth, when he questioned slyly, "You mind if I join?"

"Uh," she hesitated. She rushed to hide her razor. No matter how long they had been married, she felt there were just some things that should be kept private. Shaving in front of her man was a no-no, in her opinion. "I'm finishing up now, actually. So, hurry."

Like an excited child, he stripped of his basketball shorts and then stepped in with her. He grinned immediately, taking in her glistening curves, flushed face, and the messy bun she'd placed her hair in. He pulled her to stand in front of him and then planted the sweetest kiss on the nape of her neck, eliciting a shudder to run through her body. Jalen reached for his body wash, but not before massaging her wet shoulders.

"Morning, sexy."

"Morning to you, handsome."

She giggled like a schoolgirl and threw a handful of water at him. This would ensue a wrestling match, and she was looking forward to it, as silly as it sounded. God had completely remade their marriage and communication, and things were looking up.

Just last month, he had asked Sister Alicia to leave the ministry, and all of his extramarital affairs had been shut down. Shay had fallen off of the face of the earth miraculously, too. Jalen promised to put forth the efforts to spend more time with her, and she asked God to give them a son by the year's end. She could not have prayed for anything else. If God never blessed her again, she would be satisfied with Jalen's changed behavior.

"You trying to start something?" Jalen pressed her body against the shower wall with his. She could tell his eyes were playful and flirtatious by the way they sparkled. His palms were on either side of her head, boxing her in, or so he thought.

Jamaika ducked under his arms, carefully maneuvered around him, and slipped out of the shower. "Hurry up! We don't want to keep the photographer waiting."

His groans of dismay followed her as she wrapped herself in her robe and settled before her vanity mirror with its recently installed LED lights. As she applied her makeup, she could not help but to stare at the stunning image before her. While her lighting was topnotch, Jamaika knew her glow came from another source.

Her skin was especially clear and beautiful, and her eyes were smiling. Even her cheeks were rosy, and she had yet to apply blush. She looked content. She looked renewed. She looked...

"Happy."

Jamaika winked at herself, and thanked the Man above. He was the Healer of all, the Redeemer of all, and He had not forsaken her in her darkest hour. They were going to work, and she was SURE of it.

Hours later, at the photography studio, they separated the moment they stepped through the door.

"Okay, Mrs. Owens." The escort waved a hand in her direction. "Your dressing room is this way, dah'ling."

Jalen had been whisked off in one direction of the photography studio, and now it was time for Jamaika to get last-minute touchups and wardrobe adjustments.

She offered a hand as they walked side by side. "Thank you...?"

"Call me Pierre. Pierre, with the derrière," the intern, no older than 18 or 19, joked.

It was then that she took notice in his backside adorned with bedazzled jeans. She was tickled at both the audacity and flamboyancy of the youth nowadays.

"Thank you, Pierre," Jamaika said.

She settled in her room filled with snacks and other cutesy gifts. In their town, as much as she hated to say it, she and her husband were considered "local celebrities" and whenever they booked photo sessions or made reservations at most high-end restaurants, they were treated like royalty. Although Jamaika could do without the extras, she appreciated the hospitality and love offerings.

A young lady entered her room shortly after. Jamaika was helped into her gold-tone pumps, had her hair whipped up in a matter of ten Mississippi seconds, and was walking out to her position on a vintage leather couch. Jalen entered, moments later, matching her fly.

"You look lovely, baby." He kissed the back of her hand and settled beside her on the couch.

For the first shots, they posed in their traditional, church-friendly ways. Jalen would face the camera with Jamaika in his arms, or she sat in a chair as he stood behind her, posing. For the second round of shots, Jalen took solo close-ups, and she followed suit. Then they paused for a quick break and wardrobe change. Jamaika especially liked this third outfit. It matched Jalen's perfectly. How cute.

"How many more will be joining us, Pastor?" Pierre with the derrière had emerged with a clipboard in his hands and a pen tucked behind an ear.

Jalen thought for a second. "Three."

"Wait, what?" Jamaika's brows crinkled in confusion as she turned to him. "Three? Joining us where?"

He motioned around at the room. "For the picture."

Okay, now she was confused. He had told her it was a family picture, so why in the world other people were joining her, was beyond her. But before she could even form a whine, two high-pitched screams threatened to rupture her eardrums.

"DADDY!"

The pitter-patter of feet slammed against the sleek studio floors. Jamaika made room for the rug rats on the couch, just as they nosedived into Jalen's lap and began giggling uncontrollably. Her heart sank as she eyed the girls—his girls and her stepchildren; though, she had a hard time admitting or accepting it.

They were the same little girls he had made with another woman, years ago, into their marriage.

The identical twins, Summer and Autumn, hugged him tightly with squeals as sweet as honey. The results of her husband's infidelity sat before her in long ponytails and snaggletooth smiles and she could do absolutely nothing to stop it.

To any outsider, this made for a beautiful family picture. But Jamaika had no say-so or hand in the creation of these girls, and she disliked that they matched her exactly. Jalen had planned everything, down to what they wore, and he had not run anything past her. She was instantly irritated.

"Is there a problem?" Jalen, who noticed her smile subside, had some nerve asking such a question.

Both Summer and Autumn turned to her, and she offered a fake smile. Her insides were warming with anger and disappointment, but they were only children. They had not asked to be conceived by a married man and his mistress. They didn't deserve the hatred that Jamaika naturally felt in her heart for them.

"No, everything is fine." She did a mental countdown in her head. "But who is the third person?"

Someone at the door cleared her throat and Jamaika lost it. "Are you kiddin' me? No. NO!"

"Jamaika, stop being dramatic. We've decided to finally take this thing public." He shrugged. "I figured now was as good as time as any. Why are you trippin'?"

"YOU decided to take what public? Ooooh, your infidelity? Your babies' momma and your kids? Got it. Move! MOVE!" Jamaika stood up and brushed past the girls' mother, Rochelle. She, too, had on colors that mirrored their outfits. This intimate and beautiful photo shoot had quickly become a circus. "I'm not going to be a part of this, Jalen!"

"Hey, Africa! Where you goin', girl?"

She ignored the conceited grin on the face of the woman who had given her husband the one thing she never could. She also ignored the unfunny joke that had slipped from the woman's lips. Rochelle knew very well that her name wasn't Africa.

"We have some pictures to take. Come back, girl! Jealously looks bad on you," she chuckled.

Like a reprimanded child, Jamaika slammed the dressing room door, and fell to her knees in a heap of tears. She didn't care about the expensive clothes she wore, the name brand shoes she wore, or the fact that the floor wasn't as clean as it should have been. She stayed in the same spot, with her head lowered in shame. She had never felt more embarrassed or more humiliated in her life. Jalen could have at least warned her that his children and their mother would be joining them. Perhaps then she would not have felt so blindsided and hurt.

A knock sounded at the door and she ignored it, burying her face in her hands. All of her mascara was probably smeared by now. She concluded that she would look like a clown by the time she stopped, but it felt so good to cry and let it out.

The knocks continued and finally, she unlocked the door. She shielded half of her face with a hand as bright light poured in. "Yes?"

Jalen stood before her with his daughters on either side of him. "What's going on with you? Why did you leave out like that? What's the problem?"

"If you can't see the problem, Jay, then we have nothing to talk about here. You can't just spring all of this on me without asking first, or at least mentioning it. You know how crazy I looked out there with your family on the side coming in and infiltrating our photo shoot?"

"Everything's always about you, huh?" he questioned, stepping into the room.

Autumn leaned away from his side and hugged her leg. "Why are you crying, Mrs. Jamaika?"

She sighed and it caused more tears to squeeze from her sore tear ducts. The little girl's innocence made her even cuter, and that could not be denied.

She looked at Jalen and whispered, "I thought it would be you and me. These pictures are going on flyers, brochures, business cards, and billboards, and we're including them?"

Jalen nodded and she could tell he was growing more annoyed by the second. "Yeah. And?"

"And I didn't anticipate sharing the spotlight with your other family. Don't you get my frustration? It's…it's a slap in the face, Jalen. What are people going to think? No one at the church knows about them. How will that affect things?"

He kept quiet for the longest time. Jamaika kept her eyes low, not bothering to see his expression, nor did she anticipate the response he muttered.

"It was bound to come out someday. Why not now? You know what? You should be happy and grateful I'm sharing this part of my life with you. Everything's been so hush-hush since you found out 'Chelle was even pregnant, so now it's time to come out and be free. I'm tired of dodging all the questions and denying my children."

"There's nothing wrong with that at all. I'm not saying that and I'm not asking you to lie on your children or deny them, but dang! Couldn't you have just mentioned it first? That's my biggest problem. The girls, I can handle, but another woman? It's…just too much, Jalen."

Jalen chuckled softly and shook his head thoughtfully. "You know what's also too much? Your attitude and the fact that you don't trust me to handle my business—our business—is too much! I mean, come on, baby." He looked her over smugly. "Have a little class and understanding. Lord knows you can't bear any, so why shouldn't we feature my children? Let's go, girls."

Without another thought, Jalen grabbed each of his daughter's hands and walked off. Her heart dropped somewhere in her abdomen and she blinked at his back until he turned the corner. His cold words resonated in her spirit. She was disgusted by his unkind comments, but more ashamed that her body could not do what it was made to do. What was wrong with her?

Jamaika changed from the high-end wardrobe and back into the basic pair of jeans, T-shirt, and flip-flops that she'd worn over. Without notifying Jalen, Pierre, or anyone else, she snuck out of a back exit way, and caught a taxi downtown. She needed to clear her head. This was way too much for one day. It was way too much to process.

Her favorite thinking spot, a quaint coffee shop, was her choice of destination. There was only one other person inside, besides the waitress. "May I please have my usual?"

The woman gave a thumb up, recognizing her with a half-grin.

She chose a window booth and tucked a leg beneath her. Her eyes were focused on the outside world, as a million thoughts seemed to consume her. The day had gone from sunny and beautiful, to gloomy and miserable, and all she wanted to do was hit the reset button.

Jamaika added one packet of sugar to her warm beverage and sipped gingerly. "Ahhh." She took another swig and knew it was just what she needed.

The bell on the door chimed, but she kept her eyes down on the newspaper at the table. It was from last week, but it proved to be a decent read. She even discovered a recipe that she wanted to try. As she turned the page to continue the health article she was skimming, she heard a voice so distinctive that it made her heart backflip.

"May I sit with you?"

Standing before her, well over six feet, and looking just as plain as she, was Levi. "Um, sure. How's it going?"

His denim-clad shoulders shrugged. "It's going. I was out for my morning jog and saw you a few blocks down, so I stopped in."

Jamaika took in his jean jacket, cargo shorts, and striped tank top. He even wore brand new shoes that looked literally fresh out of the box. There was no way he was out jogging in such a getup. She had no time for any more surprises or disappointments and did not care to call his bluff.

"Oh."

Levi had a bagel in one hand and a banana in the other. "Would you like some?"

She untucked her leg and went back to reading the paper. "If I wanted more to eat, I would have gotten it myself."

Levi threw his hands up and seemed surprised by her wittiness. "Touché. Wow. I'm sorry to bother you. I'll leave you alone."

Jamaika caught his arm as he turned to leave. "No, no, sit down. It's not your fault. I'm just not having the best day. I apologize. Sit down." She closed her eyes in shame, and then shook her head.

He seemed hesitant to stay and eyed her carefully. "Anything I can do to help?"

She smiled and answered honestly, "A one-way ticket to Paris will do."

Levi chuckled. He smeared cream cheese on his bagel. "Hey, if I had the extra funds, I would be happy to. Anything realistic that I can do?"

Jamaika shook her head and rested her chin in her palm. "Just pray for me. That's more than enough."

He winked and took a bite of his bagel. "Now, *that* I can do."

For a while, they sat in silence. She continued reading and entertaining her thoughts on how badly the photo shoot had gone, and Levi scribbled in a small journal. Every so often, he would catch her eyes, and vice versa. Finally, he tucked his journal away in his pocket, and folded his hands in front of him.

"You look like you could use an ear."

Jamaika shook her head. "I have two ears; I'm good on the ears."

Levi chuckled. "Cute."

"I try." Jamaika mustered up a small smile, pushing her newspaper off to the side.

"Let me rephrase that. Let's talk." Levi reached out to grab her hands cautiously. "You could use a friend right now. Let's talk. You need to vent, and I have nothing better to do."

"How do you figure I 'need to talk'?"

"Three obvious ways." Levi cocked his head to the side, and she noticed a small birthmark on his neck. "Your eyes—they're extremely saddened and confused right now. Your body language—you're completely withdrawn from the conversation and don't even realize it. It's like you're closed off from the world. Lastly, your smile—that smile I remember so well from our first encounter—is hardly there. Now that I've creeped you out with my analysis, talk."

As much as she hated to admit it, the man was absolutely right. She twisted her fingers in thought. "Where should I start?"

"The beginning is always good. Like I said, I have nothing but time."

Chapter Seven

Levi was the perfect friend, and his advice stuck with her for the week. He gave her a perspective on love as a man and made sense of a lot of the foolishness that Jalen had put her through. Although there was no excuse or justification for his mental and physical abuse, he pointed out that Jalen may have been insecure and looked for love in the wrong places because of his past. Oftentimes, men who were void of real love growing up found it in multiple women for multiple reasons.

Levi challenged her to seek marriage counseling, first for herself, and then a second time with Jalen. What stuck with her most was his final piece of advice that he gave followed by a kiss on the back of her hand.

"More than anything, don't let this man steal your joy. It's okay to FIGHT for your marriage, but make sure you're not the only one in the ring."

For someone who had only conversed with her on a couple occasions, he was attentive and could read her like a book. He seemed to know a lot about relationships and women, and his suggestions were taken with gratitude and thought. She was so inspired by their talk that she decided to stop by a therapist's office, two weeks later. The woman was a married mother of three, and was one of the doctors who frequented the treatment center that Jamaika had been admitted to.

"I'm surprised to see you, but certainly not disappointed. How are you, honey?"

The woman, named Dr. Snowden, wore the brightest red lipstick that Jamaika had ever seen.

Her jet-black hair was curled in spirals that were almost hypnotizing, and she had the fairest, smoothest brown skin.

Jamaika was already comfortable around her, so there was no reluctance when she was invited to relax back on the leather chaise positioned at the center of the spacious corner office. The room smelled of several aromas. Jamaika could decipher between the lavender candles, cinnamon potpourri, and leftover latte from the local coffee shop.

"What brings you in? Are you feeling down again?"

"No," Jamaika said. "Well, at least not in that sense. It's with my husband and his abuse and the lack of attention he gives me. I've been playing the other woman role in my own marriage and I don't know what to do anymore. I am drained, Doctor."

Dr. Snowden nodded slowly with empathy. "Why do you think he's become uninterested? Do you think your suicide attempt has gotten to him?"

"Honestly, I think he would have loved for me to go through with it sometimes."

"Don't say that."

"I'm serious." Jamaika shrugged. "He literally is up and down with me. One day he's sweet and loving, and apologetic. The next day, he wants to argue, fuss, and fight, and then have his way with me. I never know which Jalen I'm getting anymore."

"That's never acceptable, Mrs. Owens."

"Oh, I'm highly aware. But after 13 years, you just learn to kind of deal with it. In my case, I have nowhere to go, and nothing to my name. Not a dime. I have no real savings or resources, and I don't necessarily want to lean on my family because I'm the one who stuck around and allowed all of this for so long. I'm just at a crossroad. So, you can kind of see why I wanted to check out," Jamaika explained and sighed.

Dr. Snowden smiled understandingly and sat back. She crossed a leg and watched Jamaika for a moment. "You see defeat, but honey, I see the perfect opportunity for a new beginning. As I tell all of my clients who have found themselves in an abusive situation, know that you are neither the blame nor the problem. This problem stems deeper than you could ever fathom and has nothing to do with you. Your offender, or, in your case, Jalen, has been dealing with issues long before he met you. He hid them well while you two dated. I mean, correct me if I'm wrong, but did you know of any of these issues when you two first met?"

"Not at all," Jamaika confessed. "He was so different. He was so full of love and life. We were both 18 when we met, and it was the greatest time of my life."

Dr. Snowden nodded. "Tell me more about that time."

Jamaika's mind and words drifted off as she thought about the day that they first met. It was the day her life had changed forever.

"I can take the next person in line."

The middle-aged cashier spoke dryly and motioned Jamaika over to stand before her cash register. The woman took a single look at her cart, rolled her eyes at the number of items there, and then paged another worker over.

"Hey, Jalen! Can you help me bag?"

Jamaika followed the eyes of the cashier. She peered off to the side at another worker who tried his best to ignore the request.

"Jay-LEN!" the cashier yelled this time. "Help me bag! Now!"

The young man looked up from putting boxes of cereal on a display and cut his eyes at the cashier. His uniform was like hers—a basic blue shirt and black apron with the grocery store logo on the right pocket—but he wore a matching blue cap towards the back of his head and colorful shoes.

He spoke with annoyance. "You know I was taking my break after filling this shelf. Can you page Scott?"

"He's cleaning up a milk spill in aisle eight."

"Tawny?"

The cashier gave a smug grin, swiping a box of tampons across the scanner. "She's on break."

Reluctantly, Jalen sighed and stepped over a few boxes, dusted off his hands, and then licked his parched lips. He peeled the dingy apron off so that he could dab the sheen of sweat that coated his forehead and then tossed it somewhere. As he approached the counter, his eyes landed on Jamaika who had been previously hidden from view.

His eyes seemed to light up and his otherwise lethargic movements picked up. He rounded the counter with intrigue. "I'm bagging YOU?"

"You're bagging my groceries," she corrected with a chuckle, blushing.

"How're you doing today?" He leaned both elbows onto the counter and grinned.

"I'm fine, even though I just got my hair done, but the rain sort of messed that up."

He perused her up and down. "It's beautiful. You're beautiful."

The cashier cleared her throat and looked back and forth between them. Jamaika blushed again, realizing that she was holding up the line, and then placed the rest of her items on the conveyor belt.

"I'm sorry."

After a few beeps and price checks, her gaze could not help but to float back over to where Jalen stood. As he packed her groceries cautiously and with care, she noticed the way his young, tight muscles bulged through his shirt. He was likely an athlete—she figured he played basketball with his height and build. She couldn't see a pretty boy like him playing football.

He must have felt her staring at him because all at once, his eyes were back on her.

She jumped from the intensity of the stare and glanced down at the credit card in her hands. Jamaika could feel him continue to stare at the side of her face as she gave her plastic money to the unhappy worker.

Still, she could not resist. "You didn't ask if I preferred paper or plastic."

Jalen, whose nametag was flipped upside down, chuckled and held his hands up defensively, "You're right. I didn't. But you look like a paper kind of girl."

"Oh yeah? How so?"

"Uh." He shrugged and shook his head. "I actually don't have any reasons or explanations. I just wanted to be cute."

"You already are. Don't overdo it," Jamaika flirted back.

He handed her the remainder of her groceries and winked. As she walked off, she could feel his eyes on the natural sway of her hips.

"Have a nice day, beautiful!"

"You too! Thank you!"

89

Jamaika made a beeline for her 1999 Ford Focus and loaded her bags inside. A permanent, silly grin remained on her face from the encounter. As she whipped around to return her cart, she screamed out because Jalen had somehow walked up unnoticed and was leaned onto another stray cart. He admired her for a second.

"You have to tell me your name now."

"Why do I have to?"

"I want to know the name of my future wife."

"Boy, I'm only 18!" she pointed out with a giggle.

"That's why I said FUTURE wife," Jalen repeated and returned her grin. He gathered the cart that she had and pushed it into the back of his. "I promise I don't bite."

"I'm Jamaika." She gave in and held out her hand. "Nice to meet you, Jalen."

Instead of shaking her hand, he knelt down and kissed the back of it. Then he stood to his full height, mounted the back of the cart with one foot, and then pushed off of the ground with the other. He went flying in the opposite direction like a child on a skateboard.

"I work evenings after five. Come visit me sometime, pretty lady!"

Jamaika glanced over to the therapist as she wrapped up her memories. She did not realize that she was crying until she looked down and saw that her blouse was spotted with moisture. She wiped her face and shook her head.

"I'm a mess."

"You're not. You're doing what any sane, emotional human being would do when thinking about the great memories that seemed to have gotten lost in the trials of life," the woman assured her. "How do you feel after sharing that? What color would you say is your heart right now?"

"I feel sad because I know it's not possible to get that back. I feel helpless like I'm waiting on something that will never happen." Jamaika wiped her eyes with the back of a hand and added, "As for the color of my heart, it ranges between black and blue. Black for sadness and blue for defeat, I guess."

"You said you feel like you're waiting on something that will never happen. That's not necessarily true. Maybe for this time and season it's impossible, but who's to say Jalen will not change his behavior in another year or two? Who's to say he will not have a change of heart in another few months?" Dr. Snowden questioned. "Even still, why are you waiting on him? Why do you feel like you have to put your life on hold until he gets it together?"

Jamaika thought about it. Honestly, she had no answer for that question.

"I guess I just feel like this man is all I have; he's all I know. I can't live, breathe, or be without him."

"You CAN live, breathe and be without him for longer than you realize. *You* just don't want to. Remember, you met him when you were 18. You survived before he came into your life and you will thrive after he leaves your life, if that's what you want."

Jamaika picked at her fingernails. "How can you be so sure?"

"Because I have counseled hundreds of women just like you. As a woman, wife, and mother, I am inclined to encourage you to do what's best for you and move forward without Jalen. As a therapist, my final advice to you regarding your marriage is to try this one last assignment."

"What's that?"

"Grab a pen and paper."

Chapter Eight

Jamaika left out of the therapist's office and headed home with a much lighter spirit and clearer understanding of what needed to be done. Talking her problems out had helped significantly, and she knew that she would be able to face Jalen a little bit easier now that her emotions had been checked. She was also going to try to get him to come out for a few sessions. Until they exhausted ALL options, she decided that she wasn't going to give up on her man or her marriage just yet. Call her crazy, but she had to see it through the end.

As she drove along the highway towards their gated cul-de-sac, an easy listening station filled the insides of the truck. The roads were slippery because of the pouring rain, so she kept her speed to a minimum. The high beam headlights were on because the night was darker than normal, but thankfully, there weren't many people travelling in the same direction. Her vision was fairly okay in these conditions, but still, she made sure to religiously check her rearview mirror, her blind spots, and every other spot she could think of. At the last minute, she spotted a distraught looking woman running across the road in dark clothing.

Jamaika jerked on brakes and was, again, thankful that no other cars were behind her. She signaled and whipped the car into the furthest lane to the right. She kept her car running and her lights on as she examined what the woman's next moves were. Either she was a thief in the night escaping, injured and seeking help, or she was about to make a costly mistake.

The woman looked around, crying erratically, and mounted the fence that separated her from the highway and Lake Michigan. Jamaika's eyes widened in realization and she moved swiftly from the car over to where the woman was climbing.

"Hey! Please, don't do that!"

The woman jolted in shock and looked over her shoulder. "Leave me alone!"

"Come down from there!" Jamaika called, shielding her eyes from the rain but it was no use.

"It's too late!"

"Too late for what? What are you trying to do?"

"JUMP!" the woman cried out. "You can't help me! You can't save me. Nobody can! Just let me die in peace!"

"What's your name?" Jamaika attempted to divert the conversation and keep the stranger as calm as possible.

"Michaela," the woman answered.

She wept into her arms that were still entangled in the chain link fence. She looked to be tiring out from all of the climbing that she was doing, and she appeared to be going nowhere fast, but Jamaika had to admire her persistence. With each step and pull, her breathing became more and more ragged and her wet clothes seemed to weigh her down. The rain only made the fence slippery, so she kept stumbling.

"Why are you jumping, Michaela? Surely, your problems aren't that big, are they?"

"You don't know me or what I've been through!"

Jamaika reached out cautiously and touched the woman's leg. "Try me. Come down and talk to me."

"No, so you can call the police on me?"

"Why would I call the police on you? I just want to help a fellow woman in need. I'm Jamaika, by the way."

"If I talk to you, will you leave me alone and let me jump after?"

"Of course, I will," Jamaika promised.

At the back of her mind, she was praying that God would give her the right words to say to minister and encourage this woman. She was no older than Jamaika, in her early thirties, and was beautiful despite her smeared mascara and wild eyes.

With reluctance, the woman eased her way back down the fence so that her feet were on the ground. Jamaika wrapped an arm around the woman and held the woman close to her side. They were both soaking wet and cold as Jamaika led them back to her car.

"Here. Come sit inside and get warm."

"Why are you doing this to me? Why are you acting like you care? No one cares about me. Just let me die."

"Why would I do that? I wouldn't wish death on my greatest enemy, so I certainly wouldn't wish it on you. You're gorgeous, and I'm sure your family loves you," Jamaika said gently.

"They hate me!"

"Why do you think they hate you?"

"'Cause I lost my job. My husband is already unemployed because of a work-related injury, and my kids look at me every day wondering why we don't have what everyone else has. I cannot provide for them right now. The bills are all behind, my credit is jacked up, and we go days sometimes without a real meal. I just don't want to live anymore. This is too much."

Jamaika couldn't help but think how incredulous it was that she had just left the therapist's office, and now she was the one doing the counseling. "You had no control over your job loss, that's a fact. But you do have control over your destiny. Are you going to let this take you out or are you going to fight through this?"

"I have no fight left in me," Michaela admitted.

"Well, do you love your children?"

"Of course, I love them!"

"I know you do. Your eyes lit up when you talked about them. Just think of how devastated your children would be to find out you jumped to your death. Do you want them to grow up without a mother or in foster care?"

"No," the woman sobbed and shook her head.

"That would scar them for a lifetime. I know it may be hard for you right now, but know that another job will come your way. But your life? Once that's gone, there is no returning. Don't make that lasting mistake over a temporary setback."

Michaela seemed to understand and nodded in agreement. She held her face in her hands and continued to weep.

"Oh, my God! How could I have done that to my babies?" she shrieked.

"Shhh. Calm down. I was exactly where you were a few months ago. I was ready to take my life and end it all because I felt like I wasn't good enough or worthy enough to live. Fortunately, God saved me. I truly believe He kept me on this earth for this very moment—to meet you."

Jamaika had tears in her own eyes as she reached for the woman's hands.

"We met for a reason, and if nothing else, I want you to make it home safely and be okay. Stick around for your children because they need you more than anything. They LOVE you and appreciate all that you do, even if they do not voice it!"

"Thank you so much," Michaela said. She breathed out a long exhale and looked out of the window. "You're an angel to do this."

"I'm no angel, trust me." Jamaika smiled in gratitude. "But I would like to invite you to my church tomorrow evening. I don't know if you can make it, but if you can, please come as you are. No fancy clothes or anything special, and bring your resume. I should be able to set you up with a few people who can help you get back on your feet."

Michaela embraced her without another word. Jamaika rubbed her back and thanked God for the words that He had given her to say on the spot.

"Do you need a ride home?"

"Yes, please. I honestly don't even know where I am. My family's probably worried sick about me."

"Tell you what," Jamaika said and started the car. "I'll take you to my house for a few minutes. You can take whatever you would like from my kitchen and I'll give you a few numbers to call. Are you sure you're going to be okay once you leave me?"

"I think so. I just needed to calm down and really think rationally," Michaela said with confidence. She still looked to be in shock. "I can't believe I was going to do that. God bless you for stopping when no one else did."

The two rode the remainder of the distance in comfortable silence to Jamaika's home. Michaela, who was nestled in the leather seat, had succumbed to exhaustion and fallen asleep. Jamaika draped her cardigan over her and exited the car. It was still pouring out and brisk, but somehow God's peace made her feel warm inside and all over.

She unlocked the front door and called out for Jalen once. In the kitchen, she gathered two full totes of groceries and situated them in her trunk. Michaela remained asleep, and her head had lolled to the side by now. Jamaika smiled and thanked God again for the life that was saved.

"Jalen! Come here!"

Her husband was nowhere to be found but his car was in the driveway. She could hear nothing more than the faint sounds of thumps coming from the upstairs. He must have been playing music loudly in his office like he normally did.

She wandered up the stairwell. Just in case he was wondering why she was out and about so long, she wanted him to know all that had taken place just now.

"Jay?"

Jamaika stood in front of their bedroom door that was closed. That was unusual. Normally, it was open whether someone was inside or not. She turned the knob and peeked inside. Still nothing. She called his name a final time and rounded the corner to the master bathroom.

A shower was running, and the steam was so thick that she could barely see anything in front of her. As she pulled the curtains back completely, she received the shock of her life as Jalen stood with his back to her. A petite woman with a messy bun atop her head was kneeled down in front of her husband, and both of her hands were clutching the backs of his legs.

Jalen held the back of the woman's head with one hand and he looked to be in immense pleasure as she bobbed her neck. His free hand pounded against the shower wall. That was the thumping she had heard downstairs.

Jamaika dropped her phone and stepped back. Neither one looked up until she gasped. Only then did Jalen turn around with wide eyes and a silly expression on his face.

"Hey, babe. Uh…what's up?" he questioned coolly. It was obvious by his bloodshot eyes that he was drunk.

"Are you kidding me right now? You're really doing this in our shower, in OUR home?"

"Lord knows you don't do it, so I've recruited someone who will." He had a cocky grin on his face that she wanted to slap off. "Where have you been? Why are you home so late?"

Jamaika said nothing at first. She was in too much of a shock to articulate her next words. The woman who was on her knees stood up and wiped her mouth in shame.

"Look, I didn't know he was married."

"Whatever. He has a ring on his finger as we speak. Don't play dumb. Get out of my house before I throw you out!" Jamaika threatened.

"Do I still get paid?" she asked and gathered her undergarments that were tossed off to the side of the massive tub. She looked from Jalen, to Jamaika, and then back again. "Well, do I?"

"GET OUT!" The woman stepped from the shower and was mostly skin and bones. Jamaika could only imagine where he had picked her up. "Skinny heifer!"

Jalen continued to shower and said nothing more. Jamaika watched his silhouette and knew that if she had anything electrical near her, it would have been thrown inside of the tub with him.

She turned to leave but he stopped her.

"You still haven't answered me. Why are you coming home so late?"

"Why am I coming home late, Jay? That's what you want to know, huh?" Jamaika whipped around. She chuckled bitterly, clicking her tongue against the roof of her mouth. "Well, let's see. I was out saving a woman's life, Jalen. Something you know nothing about in the pulpit or in everyday life. I was not out doing dirt like you, if that's what you're wondering. And why does it matter anyway? You're in here with some two-dollar prostitute, letting her suck on you like a plate of neckbones. You'd better hope and pray she doesn't have any diseases because..."

The shower curtain was pulled open so swiftly that it ripped. "One more word out of you and I'm going to turn this shower off and kick you up and down this house. Do you hear me?" His tone was calm, low, and serious.

Jamaika took a step back, shook her head, and said nothing more. She turned with her head high and left out to take Michaela home.

Chapter Nine

"Baby, can I...talk to you?"

Jamaika screamed, dropping a spatula, and watching as pancake batter splattered across the kitchen. She hadn't expected any other sounds besides the sizzle of bacon grease, much less an actual voice. The house had been quiet for exactly three days, five hours, and 16 minutes since Jalen's shower escapade with the whore. Not until today had he found the courage to approach her or talk to her. In fact, like strangers passing in the wind, they had walked on eggshells and avoided each other like the plague, but enough seemed to be enough.

As she cooked a late breakfast Thursday morning, clad in shorts and an off-the-shoulder nightshirt, she felt warm hands splay across her stomach as he repeated himself. "Baby, can I talk to you, please?"

"You're talking, aren't you?" Jamaika looked around and sighed at the mess she had made. It would take forever to find all of the places the batter had reached, and the housekeeper wasn't due to come for a deep cleaning for another couple days, so she knew the responsibility was on her. "Back up a little; I need to check on my hash browns."

"They're fine. Just turn around for a second, so I can see you."

"What, Jalen? WHAT? What do you want to say? Is it that you're sorry? Is it that you're a no-good husband and you need help? Is it that you've never appreciated me, and you need to step outside of our marriage to cure whatever it is you're dealing with? I know all of this already, so what more could you possibly say? Huh? *What?*"

Jalen licked his lips, never growing angry or even faltering in how he stood and watched her quietly. Her mouth trembled with impeding tears and her cheeks flushed in embarrassment, as he remained quiet.

She huffed and went back to cooking and avoiding his stare. Finally, when she could not take any more of the silence she whipped back around and began to say something, but the look on Jalen's face was enough to stop her in her tracks. He stood with tears in his eyes, and his hands balled tightly into fists. She was alarmed as he sighed heavily, with the weight of his world on his shoulders.

"Jalen, talk to me."

"I, uh...I'm addicted to sex, and I...I don't think I can be cured."

He said nothing more, just kept his head down and his eyes on the floor between their feet. She waited a few more minutes for him to say something else, but when he remained quiet, she turned back around to the stove.

"I sort of figured that," she said gently. "It's the only thing that would explain your constant infidelity and need to be with more than one woman. There's just one thing that you said that I don't agree with though."

He moved to stand to the side of her, while reaching for the roll of paper towel on its holder. He yanked off a napkin, wiping his face.

"What's that?"

Jamaika looked over from the food, shaking her head. "You know this can be solved and you can be cured. I just feel like you're not at a place to accept it and get help. You *can* stop cheating and sleeping around. You just love it too much."

He nodded. "I do. I'll admit it. You *know* I don't want to do this to you, just like you know I don't want to hurt you, but something's wrong with me, baby."

"Let's…let's speak with someone, or reach out to a professional who can talk to you and—" Her words trailed off as he shook his head in disagreement.

"I'm damaged goods," Jalen said simply. He was usually so strong in stature and unmoving, but today, he looked fragile. She actually wanted to hold him. That's how broken he appeared in that moment.

"I'm willing to bet this stems from my childhood. Things with my mother and father. Things that happened when I was visiting my cousin's house. Things that I've never told another soul," he continued vaguely. "I know it's not healthy to continue living with these secrets and past hurts, but it's stayed with me this far."

"That's never a good idea, Jay. You say it every Sunday to your congregation to forgive, to trust God, and to cling to Him in times of trouble. Why do you think you're exempt from that same advice? You have to confront the issues before healing can take place."

"It's not that…but it hurts more to confront it than to just let it fester, like I've been doing. I guess I just need you to understand that this is me."

Jamaika was confused. She began to gather plates and silverware and place them on the table. She glanced at him incredulously. "I'm sorry, but I'm not settling for that answer. I deserve better. If I received treatment for my issues, so can you. It's only right for our marriage, and our future children. I'm not accepting the fact that you're willing to tuck these things away and take them to the grave with you. I just can't. That's not fair to me or to you."

Jalen went to the refrigerator and retrieved a carton of orange juice. He deposited ice cubes into two glasses and then filled them with the pulp-free liquid.

Jamaika pressed on, "What happened that caused this? I'm your wife. I need you to talk to me. Help me so that I can help *you*. Did...did someone touch you, or molest you, or...?"

"STOP! Stop right there!" he screamed. Juice spilled as he was topping off his glass. "Don't...don't you DARE say anything else about that! You hear me?"

Jamaika already had her answer, judging by his reaction to her questions. Most of the time, sexual predators and nymphomaniacs didn't just start off enjoying sex out of the blue. Usually, though not always, those people either experienced sexual abuse or were exposed to the act early on in some form or fashion. She had learned that over the years and knew that had to be the case with her husband. Still, she knew he was growing more and more upset, so she backed off for the time being.

"Okay. I respect it." She shrugged and started making their plates. "I'm here if you ever need to talk, okay?"

Jalen breathed deeply for a few moments, and then moved to clean up his mess. "There *is* one thing I need you to do."

"Absolutely. I'll do whatever it takes." She looked over as she piled his plate with bacon.

Jalen looked her in the eye. "I can't change, so I just need you to understand my addiction...and well, put up with it."

"If the Lord's been good to youuuu. Shout thank you!"

"THANK YOU!"

" If the Lord's been a heaaaaala, shout *amen*!"

"AMEN! Preach, Pastor!"

"If the Lord's got a blessing with your name on it...well, y'all know the rest! Shout hallelujah!"

"HALLELUJAH!"

The overweight elder who had been ordained last week gripped the microphone in his clammy hands. As he spoke, his bushy toupee had a mind of its own and shifted on his balding head.

He Lives Christian Center was on fire this morning. The choir sang with immense anointing during their song selections, Assistant Pastor Gilmore was on one accord with the Word of the house, and even the children's praise dancers had blown the socks off the front row.

"Hallelujah!" Deaconess McClendon, an 85-year-old woman, slapped fives with Jamaika and jumped up to her feet.

The organist took his happy fingers and struck a special chord that made the church erupt in praise. Ushers rushed to put a cloth over women that were bent over, and ministers prayed over the weeping souls surrounding the altar. Jamaika also leapt to her feet, adorned in fishnet stockings and open-toe heels. Joyously, she clapped to the beat of the drums, stomped in sync, and yelled in her foreign language. "Hababa-shato!"

Despite her eventful week, Sunday had rolled graciously around. As always, church was her pick-me-up, and she owed God the praise for bringing her through these tumultuous days.

"You are so good." She looked upwards and felt tears of joy brimming her eyes. "So good! Thank You, Father."

A hesitant hand on her back let her know that the hospitality team was only doing their job, and she accepted the tissue that someone passed her. Her eyes remained focused on the ceiling, and she said a prayer for her marriage, her ministry, and even her unborn children.

God would provide as He had promised. He was not a Man that He should lie, so she was confident that He would not forsake her in this transition of her life. No matter how much things spiraled out of control, she knew who was in control.

Jalen's confession and audacity stuck with her all week, and if she wasn't careful, she often found herself crying in anger and confused. He had asked her to put up with his infidelity and disrespect, as though it were a medical illness. True, she realized a while ago that he was sick in the sense that he couldn't keep his private parts to himself, but that didn't make it okay or acceptable. She had been so speechless then and now, and knew that she couldn't and wouldn't answer his requests.

After service, Jalen walked over to her with Jeter in tow. He gave her a tense, half-hug, and then bade a goodbye to the security guard. His lips touched her cheek briefly before he pulled away.

"Where are we going to eat?"

It was the first words that he had spoken to her since his ludicrous confession. Conversation, at home, had been done literally through sign language, quick eye rolls, and long stares. What confused her more was that he treated her as if *she* had done wrong.

Jalen was literally two different people and each day she had no idea who she was getting for a husband. He had shouted and sang right along with the church today, so she hoped some of the anointing had destroyed his evil yokes.

"It's your choice, Pastor," Jamaika stated. She gathered her bags and waved a goodbye to Akai. They headed to their separate vehicles, parked adjacent in their reserved spaces. "But I'm definitely hungry."

Jalen bit down on his lip while he thought about the nearby eateries. When things were on the up and up between them, she had been inspired to cook every Sunday. This week was different. It had been a stressful couple of days, and she was all for relaxing the remainder of the day.

"Uhhh." His eyes skimmed the parking lot and then landed on one of their members. The woman paused to get in the car before calling him over. Jamaika noticed it was the ever-present and ever-sneaky Malia. Jalen jogged over to her, rubbed her son's head, and then spoke to her for a few minutes. He jogged back over to where Jamaika stood in irritation. "On second thought, you have a taste for barbeque?"

Jamaika followed his gaze and rolled her eyes. "What? Oh, absolutely not. I am not going over her house."

"Why not? She just invited us for dinner."

"Why would I? That girl is up to no good, and you shouldn't want to go over a single woman's house anyway, man of God."

"She's not a girl, she's a woman," Jalen defended and threw his briefcase down. He rounded his car to look at her. "Seriously, what is your problem with Malia? You've never liked her since she joined. Is THAT the way to behave, woman of God? Since you want to throw out titles."

"There's something else I'd like to throw out," Jamaika mumbled.

"What'd you say?"

She ignored him. "Jay, you must think I'm dumb. You act like I just go around not liking people. I had no problem with her until I realized what she was up to. She didn't join church for fellowship; she joined because she's your number one fan. There's a BIG difference. I've seen the looks she gives you, and it's disgusting. She should have a little more self-respect and class."

"Oh yeah? And who are you to judge and say that? You don't even know her!"

"Oh, and you do, huh?"

If looks could kill, she would be dead. Jamaika was thankful there were still people standing around talking, otherwise she was sure he would have popped her in the lip or worse.

Jalen waved at one of the visitors walking past. His face and demeanor softened as he called out, "Good to see you, young man. God bless you!" Then he turned to her so quickly she jumped. His voice was dangerously low and full of warning as he spoke through perfectly straight and bright white teeth. "Fix your face and get in your car. I'll text you the address and I expect to see you there."

Jamaika stared at him for the longest time and exhaled. She was not even going to touch on the topic of why he had Malia's home address already. "Okay, Jay. Whatever you say."

When she turned to get in her truck, he grabbed her by the forearm and continued his threats. "Listen to me. If you get there, acting a fool, trust me. Oh, you don't want to find out the consequences."

Jamaika snatched her arm from his grip and climbed into her truck. She slammed the door and eyed him all the while she put her seatbelt on and pulled off. No matter how much she disliked this woman, she still ended up in the driveway of Malia's home, a little over 20 minutes later. She reminded Jamaika of Alicia, down to their sneakiness, hot-tailed ways, and lack of respect for other people's marriages. Their fascination with Jalen was perturbing.

Jalen arrived about five minutes later with roses in his hand, and they walked up the brick driveway together. "You don't even buy me flowers," she mumbled.

Malia had a cute, modest home, Jamaika could admit, but there was no reason for them to be there. Malia was one of those women who could be powerful if she got herself together. Instead, she loved depending on others and taking what was not hers.

The door opened and Jamaika stood back, while Jalen hugged the young woman and casually brushed his hand along her backside.

"Good to see you, as always."

Malia giggled coquettishly. "Good to see you as well, Pastor." She looked up at Jamaika who was not impressed, and her smile faded. "First Lady, I didn't know you were coming too."

"Surprise, surprise," Jamaika said. "Which is funny because my husband said you invited us both over."

Malia swallowed hard. "How are you?"

"I'm thirsty." Jamaika winked and motioned to the hand that was still touching her husband. "I see you are too."

"Oh!" Malia backed away and genuinely looked embarrassed. "I'm so sorry. I…didn't mean to…"

Jamaika put her hand up, as did Jalen. He spoke for the both of them. "First Lady is just a little tired. Where would you like these roses?"

She led them into the kitchen and Jamaika noticed how Malia put an extra twist in her hips while showing them around her home. Jalen walked around as if he knew the place, and even played with her young son who was comfortable with him. Jamaika was sure that he had been over more than once to lay hands, and not in the traditional sense.

They sat down to eat ribs, corn succotash and baked beans, and Malia and Jalen talked each other's ears off. Jamaika made friends with the toddler, and was more concerned with finishing her food than entertaining, so they could leave.

"Well, it was so good to have you two over," Malia announced. She stood in the doorway with her son on her hip. "Definitely come back some time."

"Yeah. Thanks." Jamaika waved only out of cordiality and walked to sit in her car.

Jalen stuck around to talk to Malia for a few more minutes before walking down the driveway to lean into Jamaika's open window. She was sure that he was going to take advantage of driving separately, and he would probably leave here and go lollygag somewhere else.

"See. That wasn't so bad, was it?" He flicked her nose playfully.

Jamaika dodged his hand and fastened her seatbelt. "It wasn't so good, either. You two barely talked to me. It was like I wasn't even there."

Jalen exhaled hard. "See, there you go again being sensitive. You could have spoken up. You're a grown woman, Jamaika. You're older than Malia, for crying out loud. Please don't do that."

She did not want to provoke an argument, so she allowed him to rant on and on about how petty she was being. By then, Malia had gone in, but Jamaika was sure that she was looking outside and wondering why they had not pulled off yet.

"You listenin' to me?"

"Yes, Jay."

As she looked out the window, beyond her husband's head, at the quiet neighborhood, she caught the flash of a silver Mercedes Benz S-Class coupe as it zoomed off down the road. It was familiar. It was distinctive. It was…

Jamaika whipped around to observe the license plate. "Levi."

"What was that?" Jalen looked back at her while he headed for his car.

Jamaika knew she wasn't crazy. She shook her head to dismiss his questions and said the sequence of numbers and letters over and over again in her mind. Just like the evening at the restaurant, and the morning at the bagel shop, she had seen his car more than enough times and knew its details pretty well.

Was he Malia's neighbor? Had he purposely driven by so that she would notice him? More importantly, why was this man reappearing in her life for a third time?

As they prepared for bed, hours later, Jamaika wrote down the license plate number in her journal and completed her entry for the day. Jalen was still in the bathroom freshening up and humming some tune. She remembered many years ago, when they were newlyweds, and she would wait in anticipation for him to come from his shower so they could cuddle, or watch a movie.

Jalen was a jerk most of the time, and she did not understand him anymore, but a piece of her wanted her husband back. She wanted his embraces and kisses. She wanted the romance back. She wanted him to look at her like she was the most beautiful woman in the world. Their recent visit down lover's lane was short-lived and she hated that things had gone downhill so quickly.

Jamaika heard his electric toothbrush start up, and knew she had another two minutes to spare. It was time to put the therapist's assignment to work. She jumped up and changed from her long nightgown to a shorter, lacier one. She even shimmied into a pair of her favorite high heels. Perhaps he would notice her curves more and long to touch her. Perhaps she could be the reason he said goodbye to the Malias and Alicias, and homewreckers of the world for good.

As he gargled, she sprayed a tiny amount of fragrance on her collarbone and wrists and sat on the edge of the bed facing him. Jamaika loosened her ponytail holder and swung her head back and forth to allow her thick tresses to flow around her face. Whatever he desired from those other women, she prayed he would see in her tonight. After all, she was his first…everything.

"Here goes nothing," she whispered to herself as the door opened.

Jalen came out in a pair of basketball shorts and nothing more. A trail of steam followed him from his shower, and he smelled deliciously masculine.

"What are you doing?" He stopped in the process of wiping his chest from any excess water.

In his eyes was a sparkle of flirtation, but then he looked towards the TV and Jamaika's hope dropped. There was a basketball game on, and she instantly knew that she could not compete with a basketball game. "Who you tryin' to look good for?"

"My man, of course." She bit on her lip and dug deep down to portray a sexy look. She stood and walked towards him to hug his waist. "You sleepy?"

He checked the clock on the nightstand. "I'm getting there. Plus, I have to be on that plane at five in the morning. No, but for real." Jalen sidestepped her and turned back towards the television. "What're you doing?"

Jamaika gave up her antics with a scoff. "Well, I was attempting to be cute. My bad for doing what wives are supposed to do."

Jalen kept silent as she quickly changed back into what she had on and fought back tears. She was beginning to realize that he was no longer worth her tears. As he settled in bed, she stood in front of him and blocked his view of the TV.

"What happened to us, Jay? Huh? Somewhere along the way, between me being the

113

best thing that ever happened to you, you lost it. I've maintained my weight, I haven't cheated...I'm lost. Where did we go wrong?"

Jalen eyed her with no remorse for his disinterest.

Jamaika motioned around them. "I keep up our home. I cook and clean when the staff's not here working. I'm your trophy when you want to show me off to your friends, but then your punching bag when you're angry. Every Sunday, Wednesday, and Friday, I'm your well-behaved First Lady as you ask me to be, and for what? What do I get out of this marriage? You still talk to other women, you don't TALK to me...you belittle me...you sling your penis around like it's a prize and..."

Jalen looked unaffected as she betrayed her own heart and broke down in pitiful, crocodile tears.

"Just recently you told me you were making the effort to love and treat me as I deserve. What happened to those promises, Jay? Huh? Why are you punishing me for things out of my control? Was that just the alcohol talking again?"

Her questions were met with silence—cold, thick silence. Jamaika chalked up Dr. Snowden's advice as a loss. She avoided his eyes as she continued to weep into the palms of her hands. Jalen moved around, and before long, she heard the door slam shut. Her ears rang at the sound as she rubbed her eyes, and stood to her feet. She went to her part of the bathroom, and splashed cold water against her face.

For the longest time, Jamaika stared at the beautiful shell of a woman who had put her life on hold for a man who did not respect her, and who had grown slowly but surely out of love. This was the same man that she had nearly taken her life over. From day one, it was never her problem or her fault that her marriage had failed time and time again. It was always about Jalen. To think, she had wasted almost two decades on him.

Jamaika looked to her ring finger, removed the striking piece of jewelry that was nestled around it, and sat it atop the sink. Its symbolism meant nothing to her anymore, and she decided she would not wear it again.

She fell into a peaceful slumber, moments later, on her bathroom couch. When she awakened the next morning, her neck was cramping, and her legs were numb. She had slept uncomfortably all night, but she refused to leave from the bathroom and lie in bed with Jalen.

A long, hot shower made her feel invigorated, before she headed downstairs for nourishment and coffee. But in the place of her Folgers coffee grinds was a small handwritten note, in her husband's sloppy cursive.

Divorce is inevitable. Forever won't include you and I. I'm sorry. –*J.O.*

Chapter Ten

"Everyone please stand as we receive the bride."

The sounds of Chiavari chairs adjusting, and feet planting firmly on the glossy floors could be heard as Jamaika waited behind the sheer curtains. She would be revealed in just a few short moments and felt her breath catch in her throat. Her grip on the custom lilac and ivory bouquet tightened even more.

One of the biggest days of her life was finally here, and the love of her life stood just a few feet away. Jamaika was half nerves, half smiles. The enchanting ball gown flowed around her angelically, and her diamond-encrusted tiara could make any Disney Princess green with envy. Her long hair had been straightened and pulled into a neat French twist with tendrils to fall against the sides of her face.

With a nod, her wedding planner and one of the ushers pulled on the curtains that would reveal Jamaika to all of her loved ones. She gasped, surprised to see most of the church in attendance, and immediately felt joyous tears well up in her eyes. As her dad held out his hand, she looked towards her groom. Jalen looked exceptionally handsome in his tuxedo, and he cupped his hand over his mouth in awe.

"She's gorgeous," he whispered to his best man.

Jamaika waved at the familiar faces in the pews, blew kisses, concentrated on breathing, and mostly recited her vows in her head. There was no turning back now; her last name would soon be changed and her life would never be the same. She could no longer depend on Mom and Dad for advice or guidance through life. Jamaika would soon have a husband to turn to, lean on, and love on.

Her childhood pastor was officiating, and wore the biggest grin on his face as she neared the altar. Her father proudly gave her away to Jalen, who now had a single tear running down his face. He looked so in love. They briefly *hugged, and together, walked up the two steps to stand before the pastor.*

"Friends and family, we are gathered here today to celebrate the very special love between Jamaika and Jalen, by joining them in marriage. The highest form of love between two people is within a monogamous, committed relationship."

Jalen winked at Jamaika. She returned the wink, her nerves slowly but surely fleeing. Her emotions were quickly replaced with an anxiousness to be with the man of her dreams. It was the same man she had fallen in love with since their first date at an upscale seafood restaurant. Although she had an allergic reaction to the calamari, Jalen had stuck with her in the hospital as she was treated and had given her his coat for warmth as they waited in the emergency room.

Jamaika had planned, stressed, and all but pulled her hair out as the last eight months of their engagement zoomed by. Now, her big day was finally here. Every detail had somehow come together, and it became the day she had literally dreamed of since childhood.

"Jamaika and Jalen, your marriage today is the public and legal joining of your souls that have already been united as one in your hearts. Marriage will allow you a new environment to share your lives together, standing together to face life and the world, hand-in-hand. Marriage is going to expand you as individuals, define you as a couple, and deepen your love for one another."

As the pastor wrapped up his speech, Jamaika KNEW forever belonged to them. Their chemistry, love for one another, sense of humor, and friendship was unbreakable. Nothing or no one could come between them after this day forward.

"To be successful, you will need strength, courage, patience and a really good sense of humor. So, let your marriage be a time of waking each morning and falling in love with each other all over again. Now, let's get to the good part, shall we?"

Jalen's vows were first, and he nervously read off of a tiny piece of paper that his best man handed him. He vowed to love her through life's ups and downs; he vowed to tell her she was beautiful everyday of his life; he promised that he would be her biggest supporter in every endeavor. He promised a lot.

Jamaika spoke next and had memorized her vows. She gave him her definition of what a virtuous woman was, and how she would be that and more for him. She promised to give him children and make his house a home. She promised to take their passion and create romance. She even vowed to go to war for him, if times called for it. Every word, spoken through her nervous lips, would be achieved.

"Jalen, will you take Jamaika as your lawfully wedded wife?"

"I do."

"To have and to hold, from this day forward, for better, for worse, for richer, for poorer, in sickness and in health, until death do you part?"

"I will."

Jamaika paused the DVD of she and Jalen's wedding ceremony. Their smiles, the love permeating their eyes, and even the way their hands intertwined were a thing of the past. Their sweet words had not been exchanged in years, and Jalen certainly had not looked at her lovingly in forever.

She pressed play on her remote. "Jamaika, will you take Jalen as your lawfully wedded husband?"

"I absolutely do." The crowd awed.

"To have and to hold, from this day forward, for better, for worse, for richer, for poorer, in sickness and in health, until death do you part?"

"I will."

All the money that had gone into the day, all the affirmation from loved ones, and the vows…oh, how the vows were a lie. He had broken just about every commandment and went back on every promise he laid before the altar that day. Not that she was perfect, but she had never cheated on him or intentionally hurt him. She had never given up on their union.

Until recently.

"Jalen, I know you've been looking forward to this moment. You may now kiss your beautiful bride."

Amongst whistles, cheers, and claps, the two leaned in towards one another and shared the sweetest, most romantic kiss they had ever experienced. Jalen's hands cupped her face, and she hugged him closer. With his support, their bodies leaned back as though they were in a movie. They remained kissing, and eventually came up for air to jump the broom.

"For the first time ever, I proudly introduce to you, Mr. and Mrs. Jalen Owens!"

The homemade video ended with them driving off in her grandfather's classic 1937 Cadillac LaSalle Opera coupe. A JUST MARRIED banner wrapped around the bumper, and ribbons and balloons were wrapped around the antenna and side mirrors.

Jamaika ejected the DVD abruptly with tears clouding her eyes. Divorce was not supposed to be in the picture, and her great-grandmother was probably turning over in her grave. She screamed and threw the digital memories across the room. When that wasn't enough, she stomped on the DVD. Just a few cracks appeared on the DVD, and she was still not satisfied. Like a madwoman, she crushed the plastic in two with her hands.

Although her fingers now bled, she felt better. She felt relieved. She cleaned up her wounds, took a few deep breaths, and willed her anger to leave. She had an entire house to rid of all things Jalen and she had no idea where to start.

It would be a huge change now, but she was determined to keep her head high. She vowed not to fall into any depression or stupor, and knew that with time, her healing would come.

Six months later...

"That's it...seven more. C'mon, Jamaika. Give me six more..."

Jamaika pushed herself further and grunted. She was cranking out bicycle crunch after bicycle crunch. Her personal trainer kneeled beside her and looked pleased with her relentlessness. She wore compression shorts that hugged her thighs like a pair of arms, and a compression tank top that kept her breasts from spilling over with every motion.

"Who are you doing this for? Five left."

"ME!"

"And why are you doing it? Four more."

"Because I deserve to live a long, healthy life!"

"And what else? Give me three more!"

"I deserve happiness when I put on my jeans!"

"...and what else? Two more!"

"I deserve a nice butt!" She was half-joking and half-serious.

"One more. What else?"

"Plus great abs!" Jamaika exhaled while she rolled onto her stomach in exhaustion. "Whoo! You're killin' me!"

Today made exactly six months since Jalen tucked his tail between his legs and left like the coward he was. Not one word of communication was exchanged between them. An attorney had sorted out all of their legal matters and she was content with the outcome.

Jamaika was given their immaculate home, a percentage of money, and was able to keep her truck. He had paid off every bill so that she would never need anything from him, and to say the least, she deserved that much.

Life was different, but things had stabilized quickly. In spite of Jalen's abandonment, she had gained her love of life and independence, which were two things that she had lost along the way. She had completely left their ministry and joined with another. As of two weeks ago, the divorce had been finalized, and she had not shed a single tear.

Apparently, Jalen had moved on with his children's mother, and their family of four was seen everywhere around the city. He had come out publicly about his children and mistress, and much of the community appreciated his honesty and still supported him. He could literally do no wrong. It was quite the slap in the face, and at the same time a relief for Jamaika. Her happiness was long overdue, and she looked forward to the second chance at life that God had awarded her.

Other than her parents, her circle of loved ones still knew nothing about the divorce other than what they heard around town, and she wanted to keep it that way for as long as possible. She was tired of her business being in the streets, in the local magazines, and in the mouths of people who knew nothing about her. She just wanted peace from the madness.

"Good girl. Now let's do some burpees." Her trainer grinned, knowing she hated that particular activity. "What was that?"

Jamaika's cringe turned into a fake smile as she said, "I have no complaints, Ty."

"I thought so. Let's get it." She got into position and inhaled deeply. Although she disliked the way they made her feel, her body was reaping the benefits of the strenuous movements. "Just give me ten burpees, and we'll take a break. Does that sound like a plan?"

Jamaika nodded and effortlessly executed her set. As he counted down leisurely, she thought of how good she would look in her one-piece bikini. She and a longtime girlfriend were going to Fiji to celebrate the single life in a little over a week.

"Get some water, and meet me back on the mat in five," Ty instructed and threw her a towel. He wiped his own face and then walked out of his private studio for a moment.

Jamaika downed the lukewarm water as though it were her last drink on earth. It slid down her throat refreshingly, and she poured the remainder on her head. She had another ten minutes left of training and looked forward to the shower that awaited her.

Her trainer appeared with a couple free weights and placed them on either side of her feet. "You ready for the last round?"

Jamaika bounced on her tiptoes to psych herself out. "I was born ready! Fiji isn't ready for me either!"

"Let's do it!"

Turns out, Fiji was truly not ready for her. It was just as stunning as the pictures. Jamaika had a window seat while her friend, Nadia, sat near the aisle. The plane ride was just short of 14 hours and Jamaika was anxious to get into the sun and sink her toes into the beautiful white sands of Natadola Beach.

"Girl, you see this view?"

The pilot had just promised them a landing soon, and the runway grew closer and closer. As the palm trees, and clear, blue-green waters came into view, excitement from all of the tourists was apparent. When her question went unanswered, she looked over at Nadia who had literally sunk down in her seat and was all but crying.

"Oh, my goodness. Is it that bad, girl?" Jamaika questioned and tried not to laugh.

Nadia side-eyed her and exhaled as though she was going into labor.

Jamaika rubbed her friend's arm. "We're almost there. Take deep breaths. Just think about the fine swim instructors that await us."

Nadia left her state of panic and smiled mischievously. "You're right. What am I trippin' for? Our future husbands could be in baggage claim."

Jamaika looked back towards the hues of exotic greens and blues below. "Girl, I'm going to embrace this singleness. *Your* husband may be there, but I am fine. Jamaika Higgins is just fine."

The way her maiden name slid off her tongue caused her insides to warm a little bit. It felt weird not to say Owens after so many years, but it was relieving to be able to have that part of her life back.

With the help of some kind islanders, they were able to find their luggage and shuttle without hassle. The Paradise Island Hotel & Villas was heaven on earth. For the next week, Jamaika and

Nadia would be stress-free, work-free and without any agendas other than to relax and enjoy one of the world's greatest wonders.

"Is this for real?"

For miles and miles, all they saw was sand, sun, and seashells.

"It is, girl…it is! Oh, my gosh. It's beautiful," Jamaika mused.

She felt like a child at Disney World, and knew that all the months of saving up were worth it. Neither woman had done any real travelling together, other than one Cancun trip during their senior year in college. All other trips had been for missionary purposes with Jalen, and most of the time, she had been cooped up in a hotel room.

Nadia was one of those friends who were hardly around because of a chaotic work schedule, but the loyalty, trust, and genuineness never left. No matter the distance, Nadia always had Jamaika's back and vice versa. Immediately following the divorce, and before loved ones were even aware, she had come to Jamaika's bedside with butter pecan ice cream and a judgment-free ear. She was saddened to know that Jamaika had endured all of that foolishness for so long but was glad that her friend could finally move forward in her truth.

"So, what are we doing first? Where's that little itinerary I made?"

Nadia pulled her face from the satin curtains where an oceanfront view greeted them.

"Ummmm. Girl, seriously? We are NOT following an itinerary! We're in Fiji. If we want to go skinny-dipping at midnight, we can! You're with a former party animal. We're about to turn up and relive those days…"

"Oh, I remember all too well," Jamaika said with a chuckle. She reminisced on their younger days, and fell back lazily onto her plush bed. "Thank God for maturity and salvation, is all I'll say to that. You were much worse than me, might I add."

The two giggled like schoolgirls, and Jamaika knew that she had picked the perfect companion for such a trip. Forty-two minutes later, they were heading down to the restaurant connected to their villa, and the wonderful smells of islander cuisine met their nostrils.

It was pretty crowded, as tourists enjoyed this Fourth of July weekend. The sky was lit up with fireworks and added to the ambiance of the restaurant. Both laughter and music filled the night air and could be heard from miles away, as others lounged on the sand.

"Is it just me or is everyone looking at us?" Jamaika asked shyly.

She looked towards Nadia, who had danced her entire way to the maître d' booth.

"Girl, don't play with me," her friend commanded and nudged her playfully, "You mean, they are looking at *you*. You look absolutely fierce tonight."

Jamaika accepted the compliment, although she had literally just thrown on a new dress that she had gotten and called it a day.

The emerald, chiffon fabric was tight enough to complement her backside and much smaller waistline, but loose enough so that she could comfortably move around. Its neckline was lower than she normally wore but looked tasteful against the curve of her breasts. Her many circuit trainings

125

with Ty had paid off, and she was excited to show off her weight loss.

Just for Fiji, she had done something different with her hair. Instead of her naturally wavy hair that hung just below her bra clasps, she had gotten reddish, faux dreadlocks. They touched her waistline, and each time she moved, they swayed rhythmically. Lastly, her fingertips were manicured and trimmed to perfection with a vibrant gold polish. She could admit, she felt confident and beautiful.

"Thank you."

"Absolutely." Nadia leaned over and whispered, "Embrace it."

With the suggestions from their college-aged waiter, Kadema, they ordered jerk chicken skewers with pineapple yogurt dip to share, and enjoyed nonalcoholic hibiscus punch. For dessert, they munched on a summer berry trifle. When Kadema came back around with their bill, he leaned in and pointed down near the shore.

"That gentleman paid your tab, madams."

Both women looked out at the sea of people, all talking, laughing, and dancing. No one in particular could be made out in the darkness. Jamaika looked at their bill for $56 and wondered just who had spent his hard-earned money on them.

"Who is it, exactly?"

"He wants to remain anonymous. It's been my pleasure serving you, ladies," Kadema spoke politely and bowed.

Nicola tucked a generous tip in his hand. "Thank you, again, sweetheart!"

Jamaika looked out into the distance again, and was still confused by their secret admirer. "Girl, who do you think it could be?"

"No idea." Nicola stood up quickly, and adjusted her shimmery, black romper. "But I know one thing, let's get back to our room before we're followed."

Jamaika laughed and trailed behind. "Girl, stop."

"No, for real, we don't want to end up on 60 Minutes," Nadia said. She ducked her head as if she was hiding. "We're too grown to be that gullible. Don't smile at anyone and don't stop to talk to anyone. Just hold my hand and come on."

Hand in hand, the women went back up to their room, laughing as though they were at a comedy show. Jamaika undressed into her nightgown and pulled her locks into a bun. The humidity was so thick but the air conditioning in the room made her feel much better.

"What movie do you want to watch tonight?"

Nadia yelled from the shower, "Something funny. It doesn't matter!"

"Got it." Jamaika scrolled through the various channels and settled on a movie that was just beginning. Its description looked interesting enough.

Not even halfway through the movie, the self-proclaimed "party animal" was out cold. As she tucked her friend in, Jamaika whispered, "Girl, we're on vacation, there's no time for sleep."

Nadia mumbled something groggily.

Jamaika decided to walk along the shore and explore the island. She left a note in case Nadia did awaken and changed into a simple jumpsuit. The weather was still nice. It was after midnight and in the mid-70s. The stars were sparkling like diamonds

127

and gave her skin an indescribable glow. Even the ripples of the ocean waves were magnificent.

"God, You are an artist," she whispered and sat down on a boulder.

She pushed her chin towards the sky and breathed in the fresh, natural winds. It was mind-blowing how so many people were still out and about and partying this late, but this was paradise, and she could not blame them. Since the divorce, she was learning more and more to seize the day.

Jamaika was taking her life back one day at a time.

Chapter Eleven

Like all vacations, time off, or weekends, time flew by fast for the ladies. They had gone swimming with dolphins, zip lined, took a helicopter ride over the ocean, went skydiving, and even raced on jet skis. Their bucket list had gotten skimpier since landing in Fiji, and neither wanted to leave the tropical paradise. With less than 16 hours before they were to report to the International Airport, they decided to have a final dinner aboard a yacht.

This was by far the hottest day of the trip, so maxi dresses were out of the question. Jamaika wore her highly anticipated one-piece, while Nadia opted for a bikini. Both accessorized with a sheer cover-up and wedge sandals.

"Girl, I'm going to be a nice shade of charcoal when we return."

"I know, right?" Jamaika looked over the menu at her friend. "Hey, do you see anything you want?"

Nadia was silent and her dark eyes were somewhere off in the distance. "I know exactly what I want."

Jamaika shook her head, knowing her friend was gawking over some man as usual. She looked back to the menu, and her eyes narrowed in on her entrée choice.

"I think I'm going to go with…"

"A six-foot slab of chocolate? Let's toast to that," Nadia declared and stood up. She held her arms out.

"Girl, what are you talking about? What are you doing?" Jamaika questioned and as she was turning, her face was met with a large bouquet of peach and white roses. Smatterings of Baby's Breath were in the center.

"The heck? I thought those were for me, handsome," Nadia mused and sat back down. She crossed her legs and playfully pouted.

"Although you are gorgeous," the man spoke towards Nadia, but his attention was focused solely on Jamaika. "I actually know this beauty here. It's good to see you, beautiful."

Standing in the flesh, suntanned, and sweating slightly was the man she never imagined running into, especially thousands of miles away from home.

"Levi! Hey! What are you doing here?"

"Vacationing with my cousin."

The two hugged like old friends and lingered just slightly as he kissed her cheek. She knew Nadia already had 101 questions and ignored her friend's hilarious expressions.

"He actually tied the knot last week, and we stayed over for their honeymoon."

"Oh, wow, well congrats to him." Jamaika extended her hand and spoke with excitement, "Levi, I'd like you to meet my good friend, Nadia. We're actually going home in the morning. We've been here for the past six days."

Levi kissed the back of Nicola's hand. "Nice to meet you."

"Same to you." Nicola's curiosity got the best of her, and she scooted over so that he could have a seat. "I just have to know where you two met."

"Out to eat," they both answered at the same time and then shared a laugh.

"Oh, *interesting*."

130

Nadia eyed them both for a long while, and then excused herself. Her eyes gave her intentions away. She was definitely up to something.

"I'm going to go get some of the shrimp from the bar. I'll be back. Jamaika, you want anything? Levy?"

"It's Levi," he corrected politely, "and no thank you, Nicole."

"It's Nadia," she answered back just as quickly. "No foot massages or butt rubs while I'm gone."

Jamaika reached out in embarrassment to hit her friend, but she had moved too quickly.

"Please ignore my friend. She doesn't get out much. But back to you. Are these flowers for me?"

"They are," Levi confirmed and pushed the plentiful bouquet closer to her. "I saw you two when you entered and wanted to do something special for you. Call me old fashioned, I know."

Jamaika closed her eyes and deeply inhaled the roses. "No, no…it makes me happy to know chivalry isn't dead."

Levi wore red, white, and blue swim trunks and was shirtless. His caramel skin had been kissed by the sun, as he appeared a shade darker than when she had met him nearly a year before.

She brought her eyes to his perfect white teeth. He wore a knowing smile on his face, and she became flushed at the way he looked at her. Suddenly, she felt naked beneath his gaze. He kept his eyes above her neckline like the gentleman he was.

"Thank you. I really appreciate it."

"My pleasure."

"I also appreciate you paying for our dinner the other night." Jamaika bit down on her lip unsurely, "At least I think that was you."

Levi played dumb for a second and then burst out laughing. "Yeah, you got me. That was me trying to be anonymous. By the way," he said and reached out and twirled her hair between his fingertips. "I like this look on you."

"Thank you."

"You look good, Jamaika." Levi caught himself as his hand moved from her hair to her face. He snatched his hand back and dropped it into his lap. "So, if I were to give you my business card, would you have lunch with me back in the States?"

Jamaika leaned back in her chair. She was surprised at his boldness.

"Why do I feel like you've been waiting forever to ask me that?"

Levi accepted a glass of water that a nearby server handed him. Before answering, he sipped slowly. She watched as his Adam's Apple moved up and down, and then he licked his lips.

"Because I have."

"I'll have to check my schedule," Jamaika spoke nonchalantly, jokingly.

She was still very aware that he was married, and despite her situation, there was no way they could be anything other than friends. Besides, she was not interested in dating. She was ready to focus on rebuilding her life and seeking God more now that her heart and mind were freed.

"I'm a busy woman, you know."

"Oh, I know." Levi winked and nursed his drink. "Especially now that you're single. I'm happy for you."

Jamaika's eyes narrowed instantly, and she became speechless. His face was serious, and his words were genuine. But how did he know she was single? They had not talked since that awkward day at the café.

"Excuse me?"

He pointed to her empty ring finger. "Lucky guess."

Before she could give a counter argument, Nadia sauntered over with two plates in her hand. They were both filled with seafood, Cajun vegetables, and exotic desserts.

"I am about to tear this up! Levy, don't judge me."

"It's Levi," he again corrected and stood up. His eyes stayed with Jamaika's as he bade a goodbye, and then smoothly tucked a business card in her limp hand. "Nice meeting you, Nicole. Sweetheart, I'll see you in the States."

"Take care, Levi."

Nadia said grace over her food and then looked back up. She was quiet all of a few seconds.

"One, I'm going to excuse the fact that he called me the wrong name."

"Like you called him the wrong name?"

"Whatever, and two, you already know what's my first question."

Jamaika buried her face in her hands.

"Can we just save it for the plane? It's the last day, girl. Let's just enjoy us."

Nadia bit into a hush puppy, and her eyebrow shot up. "Either you forgot to tell me about that fine specimen of a man, or I totally wasn't listening to you when you were talking."

"I told you about him once, but I think you were half-sleep on the phone. I never told you anything else because I honestly didn't expect him to show back up in my life," Jamaika explained.

She stood and slid the business card in her purse. She still could not believe Levi's assumptions, let alone the fact that he had ended up on their trip. She certainly had not thought about him but once or twice after that mysterious drive by at Malia's house.

"Don't think too much into it. I'm not interested on that level. He's just a friend."

"Humph." Nadia bit into a jumbo shrimp. "You just hurry up, and come back here, little lady. I'm not done with you."

Jamaika winked. "What if I want to sit with Levi?"

"Girl, please."

As promised, she spilled the beans and every bit of juicy detail she could muster up about Levi. Nadia was convinced that Levi wanted to replace any memory of Jalen in Jamaika's life, while Jamaika brushed it off as a small attraction that would never be.

Her divorce was still very fresh, so there was no rush in dating or bouncing to the next man, but Levi was extremely interesting. He was a gentleman, far past what Jalen had ever been, and he was handsome beyond words.

Moving forward, Jamaika promised herself, she would seek God in all of this and surely, Levi's purpose in her life would be revealed soon enough.

With deep dismay, she returned to work the following Monday at her cubicle. She was an assisting editor at Lisle Tribune, and loved her job, but could have used just a couple extra days off.

With Jalen, she never had to work and that bothered her. Now that she was single, she could earn her own coin and enjoy the reaping from her hard work. Her coworkers greeted her happily and asked about her tropical getaway.

"It was awesome. I miss the warm weather already."

"Did you swim with the dolphins like you wanted?" Tamara, the vibrant mail clerk, asked and sat her hip on the desk.

"I did." Jamaika leaned back in her swivel chair. "They were such friendly creatures, so gentle, and…"

Gerry, one of the managing editors, rounded the corner quickly with a paper in his hand and interjected, "Ms. Higgins, it's good to have you back in town, but I need to talk to you!"

"Hey, GG. I was actually just telling Tam that I was able to swim, snorkel, ride the…"

For the second time, Gerry interrupted her as she spoke. This time it was because he slammed a newspaper before her and demanded she read it aloud.

"This is urgent! Look at this!"

"Calm down, calm down."

She and Tamara read the headline of the paper and her breath caught in her throat.

"*'Former megachurch First Lady cashes out from divorce and bares it all in Fiji'…'New love interest, rocking a wedding ring, spotted with the recent divorcee.'* Wait, what is this? Who did this? This is *our* paper!"

"I know, I know." Gerry rubbed his forehead where a headache had likely already formed. "Some 'source' emailed it over, and the intern put it through. I'm sorry, Jamaika. She had no idea you were a part of our staff, and the editors were slow at catching it. With you being so new, your name slipped right through the cracks."

135

"In other words, my own job screwed me over?" she summed up with furrowed brows. "This doesn't make any sense. Who would do this to me, though?"

Jamaika dropped her head and read the headlines over and over again. She willed the writing to go away or somehow change before her eyes. Worse of all, her swimsuit-clad body was visible for everyone to see.

There were many images. Some were of her on the beach, lying out on the sand. One picture captured her and Nadia walking in their bathing suits, hand in hand. That same day, Nadia had suffered from extreme sunburn and Jamaika had helped to rub some sunscreen on her back. That picture had made the paper too, and after edits, it appeared that the two were intimately involved.

Whoever had snuck these pictures of her, had also done so the day before she left. Staring back at her was the exact moment that Levi reached out and touched her hair. There was also an image of her accepting flowers from him, hugging him, and him kissing the back of her hand. They looked cozy and involved, as the headline suggested.

She cringed at what her new church home and colleagues would think. She grew sick at the idea that she could lose her job over misunderstandings, obvious rumors, and assumptions. But more than anything, she wondered who in the world had written such a defaming article on her.

Chapter Twelve

Bzzz. Ding. Bzzz. Ssssssk!

There was absolutely nothing better than the sounds of a barbershop, getting down on a Friday afternoon. Guys, young and old, lined the walls. Some were ready to be seated and trimmed up, while others lingered to show off their fresh cuts and unique designs. The hot topics for the hour were sports and females from around the way. A hip-hop station played somewhere further in back but was practically drowned out by the thick male chatter and laughter upfront.

Heads turned as Jamaika entered the men's full-service barbershop that Jalen had recently opened with one of their longtime mutual friends. She had taken an off day to handle personal business and confronting him on the slanderous article was at the top of her list. She kept a low profile with the dark shades that covered her eyes. Under her arm was a small handbag that matched the lavender of her top, and in her other hand was the rolled-up newspaper she had grown to hate. Her irritation grew as she zeroed in on Jalen.

"Jay!" Her steps grew softer as she came up behind her ex-husband and tapped his arm. "Can I speak with you?"

Jalen looked up from texting and watched her through the mirror. Shock registered on his face and for a moment, he said nothing. Clearly, he was surprised to see her. He turned to face her, still speechless.

She cocked her head to the side. "*Now?*"

"Give me a sec, bro." The young barber, who was trying out some new clippers on his head, stopped and walked off without another word.

Jalen's eyes lowered to her outfit, and only then did he speak. "Wow. You look...good."

Under different circumstances, she would have taken joy in his shocked face and genuine compliment. She was positive he noticed her leaner stomach and firmer thighs. Her butt looked especially tight and perky in the skinny jeans that she wore, and her arms were well-sculpted in her sleeveless blouse.

She *knew* she looked GOOD.

On the other hand, Jalen was scruffy and had gained a few pounds. His beard was unkempt and longer than ever, and his eyes were what she could only describe as lifeless. He still didn't look as bad as she hoped he would, but she knew his day was coming. He still had some hell to pay and some reaping to do.

She shook her head to clear her thoughts so she could focus on what she came for. She shoved the newspaper into his chest. It crunched and fell before he could grab for it and look at it. "What is this?"

"You know exactly what that is, and you know what you did. *Why* you did it, is my concern. We agreed that we wouldn't throw any more mud in each other's faces." Jamaika picked the paper up off of the floor and held it in her trembling fingers. "Why are you trying to sabotage me?"

"What are you talking about? I don't know what you're referring to." Jalen stood up and reached for her hand. "Let me see what you have."

"Don't play dumb! You know EXACTLY what this is!" Jamaika gave up the battle of cordiality and slapped him with everything inside of her body. She was not sure where it came from or where she had gathered the audacity, but he deserved it. "Why, Jalen? I have done nothing to you!"

Some of the men in the waiting area *oohed* and *aahed*, while others began whispering like excited high schoolers. It was all over town that the two had split up, and this was their first encounter since the divorce. She was sure people would take pictures or partake in some gossip because of it, but she did not care. She was hurt. Jalen had crossed the line with this article.

He gritted his teeth and snatched the smock from around his neck. He motioned for the young barber to return to the now empty booth.

"I gotta holler at her for a sec. Keep anybody from coming to the back."

And holler he did.

The moment Jalen was behind the thick Plexiglas, the palm of his hand swept across the tops of the counters and knocked everything down. Jamaika stumbled back several feet and attempted to run from his wrath. He wasn't stupid. He would never publicly hit her or cause a scene, but she could never be too sure. He had become such a monster.

Jalen punched the wall with so much force that she was sure his knuckles would be raw for weeks. A nice-sized hole was left in the wall, and that seemed to further upset and piss him off. He growled as he turned around and his eyes locked on her. When he charged towards her, she grabbed the nearest thing that she could find. She reached for the broomstick and raised it towards him in defense.

"You must be feeling cute or something, but whatever the case may be, never in your life will you talk CRAZY to me in front of my people, in my shop. Am I making myself clear?"

Apparently, she did not answer quickly enough because he snatched the broom from her and then cornered her. "Do I make myself clear, Jamaika?"

"Jalen, first of all, back OFF of me." Jamaika pushed against his chest until he backed away some. "You don't scare me anymore!"

"I'm not trying to scare you! I'm trying to figure out what's wrong with you?" He threw the broom down, stepping back slightly. "You slapped me!"

"You've done a lot worse to me. You'll survive." She wanted to crack a smile at the handprint she left on his face.

"What's wrong with you?" he asked again.

"What's wrong with me is this." She held up the paper. "What did you do, Jalen? What is this?"

"What is what?"

"READ IT!"

She gave him the newspaper and sat down on one of the stools. She breathed in and out deeply as he skimmed the first page. His eyes widened and his expression genuinely looked shocked as he glanced back up.

"You think I did this? I didn't even know you were going out of the country!"

"Uh huh. Sure, you didn't." Jamaika stood up and headed towards the door. "You know, the funny thing is, I expected you to retaliate or find a way to make me look like the villain. But I never expected this degree of evil. You realize I can lose my job over this, right?"

"Why would I write an article like this?"

"I don't know. Why would you?" Jamaika threw her hands up in defeat. "I don't know what's going on, or what I did to deserve the way you treat me, but I'm done, Jay. I'm tired. Why don't you just leave me alone? We're divorced and I owe you nothing."

Jalen continued to look at the paper as he shook his head. His brows were crinkled in confusion. "Jamaika, seriously, I did not do this."

She was not sure what to believe as she crossed her arms.

He pointed to the paper. "Who's that guy anyway?"

Jamaika shook her head in disappointment and opened the door. "That doesn't even matter right now. Jalen, I hope you know that of all the things you've done to me, this is by far the LOWEST."

"Jamaika…"

"I hope you rot in hell," she said and slammed the door closed.

All eyes were on her as she ran to the car and sped off down the road. Of course, she did not expect him to admit his wrongdoings, but she was hoping for at least an apology or reassurance that he would make things right. All week, her job had been working with local newspaper firms and media stations to clean up Jalen's mess.

Nadia had been calling with concern and she felt bad that she could do nothing about the incident. Even her family in other cities contacted her. Jamaika was nearing rock bottom all over again.

She dropped her head in her hands at a stoplight and told herself she would not cry.

141

Although tears did not make her weak, lately, she was not feeling strong at all. True, people like Akai and her parents had called to check in on her, as well as her brother, but she still felt incredibly lonely. There was a sadness she could not shake. She wished she had a beautiful baby to run home to and hug, to escape from the malice of the world. She suddenly remembered the business card in her purse.

Since receiving the card, she had always brought it along with her. She carried it close, just in case of an emergency. Without a doubt, *this* was an emergency. Ten numbers were dialed beneath her manicured fingertips.

"Leviticus Daniels speaking."

Jamaika jumped at his voice. It was so commanding and confident.

"Um, hey, Levi." She cleared her throat, nervously. "This is…"

"I was hoping you called," he whispered, and in the background, she heard other voices. She could tell that he was smiling. "How are you? Is everything okay?"

"Not at all."

"What's wrong, sweetheart?"

She bit her thumb nail for a second and was afraid to verbalize her next words. "Hey, are you busy? I need to talk to you."

He excused himself. She could hear a door close, and then silence. "What's up?"

Jamaika braced herself for the rejection. "I know you're married, but as a friend, I need you right now. Can we please meet face to face? I really need to see you."

Levi knew that this was serious. He promised to leave a business meeting right away and meet her at his condominium complex, not far from where she was. Less than 12 minutes later, he pulled up beside her truck.

"Hey, park in my garage."

She texted Akai and Nadia her whereabouts in case he did turn out to be a psychopath and followed behind him inside his roomy, contemporary home. It was the epitome of a bachelor's pad complete with empty, white walls, and no curtains over his expensive looking window blinds. His furniture and appliances were lots of blues, blacks, and greys. Even more surprising, his home was spotless from corner to corner.

He volunteered to cook them an early dinner, and she was thankful because she could not remember eating today. The newspaper fiasco had her stomach in knots and naturally, she was unable to consume anything. Effortlessly, he moved around his kitchen, with an apron around his lean waist and he changed from his business attire to basketball shorts and a tank top.

Without breaking a sweat, he made homemade noodles for their spaghetti. He seasoned and kneaded the ground turkey with his smooth hands, and even made a special batch of dough for the garlic bread.

Occasionally, he would offer her a spoonful of tomato sauce to taste, or he would stir around in the pot and come away with a noodle or two. He was married, and she was still finding herself, but he looked good. It was a *wish-he-was-single* kind of good.

As he brushed butter along the tops of the bread, he looked over to where she was quietly watching.

"So, I know you didn't just come over to get a free meal."

Jamaika smirked.

"Where's that beautiful smile I'm used to?"

She forced a grin.

He shook his head and placed the pan in the oven. After setting the timer, he walked back to where she sat and gently nudged her. "That's not good enough. We definitely have to talk. What's going on, Jamaika?"

She took a deep breath and stared back at him. Genuine concern was painted on his face, and she could feel herself melting. Either that, or the kitchen was too hot.

"So, that day I came back from Fiji, my boss handed me this." Jamaika sat the newspaper on the countertop. "Needless to say," she continued and buried her face in her hands, "it has pretty much turned things upside down for me, because some idiot sent one of the new editorial interns this story, and she put it through. She didn't even realize I was one of the staff members, and now this entire thing could cost me my job. I just can't seem to catch a break."

Levi was silent as he examined the front page of the newspaper.

Jamaika continued to explain. "I confronted Jalen about it, but he of course denied it. I know it was him. Who else who want to sabotage me?"

"They got your boy in it and everything, huh?" Levi admired the black and white photograph.

"Yes. I am so sorry." She dropped her head onto her folded arms. Even with her head lowered, she could feel him reach for the paper and finger through it. "I hate that they dragged you into it."

He cleared his throat and placed the paper back down. "Why are you apologizing? I can definitely fix this."

Jamaika lifted her head. "You can? How?"

Levi went to the refrigerator and took out a bottle of sparkling apple cider. He pulled two glass flutes from the cupboard and set them before her. Cockily, he shrugged.

"Absolutely. That's nothing to a boss."

"How can you be so sure?" Jamaika accepted the cider and sipped it slowly. He was so confident. "What do you do, exactly?"

He winked at her and went to check on the bread. "Just trust me."

"Okay," Jamaika agreed and returned his smile.

Not knowing what any of this meant, or even what he did professionally, she decided to leave it in God's hands and revisit the damage another day. She owed it to herself to just enjoy the night and let go of her frustrations if only for one night.

They ate dinner with the sounds of smooth jazz softly playing throughout his living room. His food turned out to be delicious, and apparently, it was a special family recipe that he said he would reveal to her only if they were to get married.

"I guess I'll never find out," Jamaika laughed. She twirled the pasta onto her fork and looked around. "You have a beautiful home. How long have you lived here?"

Levi squinted one eye in thought. "Mmm...two and a half years. Not that long. I know it looks bare," he chuckled.

She pointed to the only picture frame in his house. "And your wife? It literally looks like a single man's home. She didn't have her hand in anything, did she?"

Levi chuckled again and stretched his arm to grab the bowl of Parmesan cheese. He had grated a fresh block of it before sitting down.

"No, she had no hand in it. This was all me. I think she'd be proud of my decor though."

"*Would be* proud? Have you two separated?" Jamaika watched as he grew uncomfortable and looked off into the distance. "You don't have to answer that, if you don't want."

"No, it's fine," Levi assured her. He sipped some cider before speaking, and she noticed the way his eyes glazed over with tears. "My wife passed away."

Jamaika closed her eyes. "Oh, no."

Levi shook his head in remembrance. "Yeah…well, she was killed in a car accident. A drunk driver hit her head-on and fled the scene. I didn't find out until she passed in the hospital that she was 22 weeks pregnant with our daughter. The doctors did everything they could to save her, but God saw it fit to take them home."

Jamaika's hands went up to her mouth and she regretted ever being so inquisitive.

"Oh, my goodness, I am so sorry! I should have put the pieces together. Me and my big mouth!"

He smiled sadly and stood up to leave out of the room. A single tear rolled down his cheekbone and puddled at the corner of his mouth. Without thinking, she stopped him from walking with a hug. She nestled her face in his chest, and his chin settled atop her head. She knew what it felt like to lose a child and she was sorry that she had ever said anything.

For the longest time, they embraced. Levi openly cried and she imagined that this was the first time that he had gotten a good cry. They moved from the dining room table to the living room couch. Their bodies were inseparable.

She rubbed her hand back and forth over his warm back, whispering, and praying his strength. Little by little, she felt the tension leave his body and he seemed to calm down after a while.

She could not help but to chuckle at God's sense of humor. Here she was, longing for Levi to be her comforter and the mender of her problems, but it was Levi who needed it most. They talked all night.

He opened up about growing up with a single mother, who had also been killed in a car accident. He reminisced on how low he felt, and it seemed that déjà vu had hit him over the head when his wife and daughter had been taken from him. He even shared how he had considered suicide, and thanked God for the blank bullets in the gun that he had used.

Jamaika shared her own testimony of nearly ending her life. She told him about Jalen's abuse and adultery, and how her parents were completely wrapped up in him—until recently—despite her unhappiness. The two talked about their hopes and dreams and biggest fears. They were much more alike than she imagined, and she could easily talk to him for hours. He was such an articulate, good looking, gentle and considerate person. Jamaika truly envied his future wife.

"Wow, it's almost midnight." Levi checked the clock on his mantle. Time had truly flown by. "Come on, I'll trail you home. Where do you stay?"

Jamaika stood up and stretched. "Oh, you don't have to. I'm only 20 minutes away on the freeway."

"*Only* 20 minutes away? That's a definite no-no, by yourself." Levi got up and went down one of his long hallways. He came back with a blanket and pillows. "Or did you want to crash here? I promise I won't bite."

Jamaika swallowed hard and weighed her options. She definitely didn't want the night to end and would gladly curl up on his comfortable couch. She was exhausted and she trusted him. On the other hand, she didn't want to appear a certain way to him and prayed to God that he was as genuine as he sounded. There was always the pepper spray in her purse if anything got too crazy, plus she knew a little taekwondo.

"Um, sure."

"If it makes you feel more comfortable, you can lay in my room and lock the door."

"No, no, it's fine. Thank you for everything," Jamaika spoke sincerely and hugged a pillow to her chest. "I enjoyed our talk. I really mean it."

He extended his arms and hugged her. He smelled so masculine; it was a mixture of pure testosterone, traces of body wash, and cologne.

"I enjoyed you too. You came at a perfect time in my life."

She backed away slightly and held his face. It was a scene straight out of a movie the way time stopped. Jamaika did not blink, and Levi kept his gaze on her.

"You are breathtaking," he whispered.

She hoped that her breath was not too offensive from the garlic and onion from dinner, as he slowly leaned in to kiss her cheek. His lips pecked there once and then twice, and then their lips found one another in a slow, passionate dance. They became so close that she could feel his heartbeat against hers.

They were so in sync that as he breathed, she inhaled his same precious air. His hands fell to her hips, holding her against him. Her fingers rubbed the nape of his neck and drew him closer. Jamaika prayed that he never let her go.

It felt right. It felt heavenly. It felt natural.

Levi was the first one to pull away, and it was to admire her with a soft smile on his face. He watched her with sleepy eyes, and then pressed his forehead to hers. "I think that's my cue to let you sleep."

"I think so too." She leaned on tiptoes one final time as they kissed.

"If you need anything, I'm just right up the hallway," Levi assured her.

He dimmed the lights and tucked her in. He placed the remote beside her and made sure all of his appliances and stove were off. She watched him until her heavy eyelids dropped.

With peaceful dreams and positive thoughts, Jamaika slept like a baby. She awakened the next morning to the delicious whiffs of bacon, blueberry muffins, and fresh fruit. Levi was on a phone call with his back facing her, so she scurried off to the bathroom where a drying towel, washcloth, and other hygienic necessities awaited.

She smiled at his thoughtfulness and showered. Thankfully, she did not have to be at the office until later this afternoon so she could enjoy his breakfast and conversation. Unashamedly, she had thought about him much of the night, and even in her dreams.

"When did you get up?" Levi asked as she peeked her head around the corner. "Whoa."

Jamaika was wrapped tightly in a towel with her damp hair glistening and combed around her face. The tops of her shoulders were painted in moisture and for the first time, he noticed the tiny freckles on her cheekbones. Unable to help himself, his gaze dropped to her perfectly shaped legs and painted toenails.

"Levi?"

"Uh, yeah?" He cleared his throat and finally turned away from her. He said a silent prayer for strength and control.

"May I borrow some clothing?"

He directed her to one of the closets in his bedroom. As much as she didn't want to snoop, she did. Levi was neat and had straightened his bed this morning. His countless shoes were all stacked neatly in one closet, and everything from his ties, socks, and loungewear was coordinated by color.

"Impressive."

Jamaika found a solid grey T-shirt and a pair of black joggers. They were baggy and much too long for her, so she rolled them down around her waist. In the bathroom cabinet was a new stick of roll-on deodorant that she found and applied to her underarms.

"This will have to do," she said and looked down in amusement.

Never in her life had she spent the night over a man's home, not even male family members. Even though they had kept things respectful, she realized how bad things would look if someone saw her leave out or knew that she had slept over. She would not tell a soul. Not even Nadia.

As she French braided her hair in two sections, she came across a business card from his workplace that had fallen to the carpeted floor. They had discussed careers vaguely, but she still had no idea what he really did. She tucked it in her bra to read later and joined him back in the kitchen where he was making her a plate at the breakfast bar.

"There she is," he said and poured cranberry juice into a glass. "I hope you're hungry."

"I'm starving." She grinned and sat down across from him. While she showered, he had added an egg, ham and red pepper quiche to the menu. "This smells really good. You sure know the way to a woman's heart."

He lifted his glass. "May we toast to new beginnings?"

Jamaika raised her own glass and tapped his. "We shall. To new beginnings."

Chapter Thirteen

Jamaika made it to work right on time. Normally, she was a half-hour early to catch up on any emails and check her mailbox, but Levi had kept her for as long as he could. They had eaten until their stomachs protested, and over decaffeinated coffee, they sat and talked for hours on his balcony. Not once had he tried anything, and she loved that about Levi. He was such a gentleman.

"I see someone had a good night," Ivanna, the newest receptionist in training, teased. She was looking at Jamaika over her red, wire-rimmed glasses with an impish smile.

"I had a good night's rest, if that's what you're implying," Jamaika challenged. The receptionist was nosey, and always had some slick remark for everyone that entered.

She waved to a few other coworkers before unlocking her corner office. Her extraordinary work ethic had landed her an upgrade from a cubicle to an office. Despite the newspaper foolishness, her boss saw it fit that she was promoted. Her integrity following the situation and the fire behind her latest articles had propelled her into journalistic superstardom.

"Oh, my." What greeted her on her desk was a bouquet of yellow carnations. They were as bright as the sun peeking through her blinds.

"They were delivered just before you got here."

Jamaika jumped slightly at the sudden interruption. Ivanna had somehow followed her into the office and was leaning against the doorway.

Jamaika rounded her desk and shooed the receptionist out of her office. "Ivanna, please get to work!"

"Who are they from?"

Jamaika opened her door wider and spoke, "Don't you have some voice messages to leave on somebody's phone, or lattes to fetch for the third floor? Goodbye, NOSEY!"

Ivanna pushed her glasses further up the bridge of her nose and crossed her arms. "Hmmph!"

The 30-year-old twirled on the balls of her feet, that were already freed from her work shoes, and marched off.

Jamaika closed and locked her door, and then sat down behind her desk. She searched for the little white card in between the carnations and though there was no sender's name, she figured it out quickly.

It read: ***Dinner at my place again?***

Jamaika beamed. She knew that Levi must have set everything up when she saw him on the phone this morning. She smelled the flowers and read the note over and over again until her phone beeped and broke her concentration.

"Ms. Higgins?"

"Yes, Ivanna."

"You have a call on line one. It's a gentleman with a response to last week's Letter to the Editor."

Jamaika rolled her eyes and finally looked away from the flowers. "You may patch him through. Thank you."

Her smile stayed with her throughout the day, even as she encountered unhappy callers from the subscription department, received the wrong

153

lunch order, and was forced to sit in on a marketing meeting for her sick boss.

She could not stop thinking about her new friend, nor could she stop comparing Levi to her dog of an ex-husband. Levi was some kind of different, and she looked forward to getting to know him better.

For three consecutive weeks, Levi either cooked dinner for Jamaika or took her out to eat. She literally had not gone grocery shopping but once and was spending more time at his house than her own. They were like newlyweds, minus the intimacy.

Each day proved to be a new adventure, and a new way to learn one another. She could honestly say she loved talking to him, and he enjoyed showering her with gifts and sweeping her off of her feet.

Jamaika could not resist and opened up about her progress with Levi to Nadia. She apparently had known since meeting him in Fiji that he was the one for her friend. Their friendship had no title, and Jamaika vowed never to kiss him or sleep over his house again, but she could say that she trusted him with her life. Their chemistry and budding friendship superseded any relationship she had experienced with any other guy previously, and it absolutely terrified yet excited her.

As promised, he had even cleaned up the newspaper mess for her, and she learned that he was a well-respected publicist for many of the big-time corporations around Illinois. The way he protected Jamaika and went to bat for her was refreshing. For so long, she had been trapped in her marriage, so this was all so new to her. A man actually wanted to be the provider, protector, encourager AND friend, with no strings attached, and expected nothing in return?

Wow. She could not wrap her mind around that concept, or the fact that Levi always went out of his way to make her feel special. She appreciated his efforts, both large and small; she appreciated the time and thoughtfulness he put into building their trust and to rescue her from any insecurities or doubt that Jalen had instilled.

What was *most* amazing was their easy, beautiful, and meaningful conversation. They could talk for hours about everything and nothing, and still manage to stay on the phone until the wee hours of the morning. Jamaika's heart soared at all of the possibilities to become of their relationship, and was in no rush to do or say anything that would hinder their growth and progress...

"Jamaika, I love you," Levi's words touched the atmosphere, softly but firmly.

He and Jamaika were seated in his leather recliner with her body leaned into his side. They were watching Family Feud, and he had been playing in her hair. Over Steve Harvey's voice and the crowd's cheers, his words were pure and echoed in her ears.

Her heart skipped a beat as she climbed on his lap to face him. Unsure if she heard him correctly, she began to speak but he shushed her.

"Listen, listen. I know it's soon and I'm not saying we have to jump into anything or make things official. I know you're still getting over your divorce and recovering from that, but I love you. I've loved you since the moment we met, and you kneed me in the groin."

Jamaika's head fell forward onto his shoulder as they laughed. She brought her head back up to look down at him, feeling warm tears prick the backs of her eyes.

"Now, I don't expect you to say it back, and you may not even feel the same way, but I wanted you to know. If no one else tells you, know that you're beautiful. If no one else hugs you, know that I will. If no one else loves you, know that I do," Levi confessed.

"That was beautiful, Levi," she whispered.

He pressed his forehead to hers and looked her directly in her eyes. "*You* are beautiful. More and more each day, I find myself more intrigued by you. It's been incredible, getting to know you, Jamaika."

She was not sure what to say, and instead, let her lips do the talking. She was not quite falling in love *yet*, but there was definitely an infatuation and an unquenchable fascination that only Levi could satisfy. She kissed him once, then twice, and then a third time. His arms encircled her waist and held her in place as he reclined backward and continued kissing her.

They ignored the game show. Their bodies still touched, and their hearts still beat as one. Only when his phone buzzed at his hip, did they break apart slowly.

"That may be important," Jamaika pointed out while she backed away from him.

"Don't leave. Stay with me," he encouraged, and then cleared his throat. He licked his beautifully sculpted lips and lowered his voice to a more professional tone. "Leviticus Daniels speaking."

As he talked, she played with the nape of his neck. She tried not to eavesdrop, but the caller was oddly loud and frantic, and Jamaika was close. She turned back to the TV, but her attention was on

156

Levi, as he told the woman on his end that he was busy.

When the woman continued to talk, he spoke over her, "Can this wait? I'm actually with my friend right now. Besides, I told Ross I was no longer in charge of that piece, and I wanted all the information wiped out. I gave it to you for a reason."

The caller sighed and mumbled an explicative.

"I understand you handed me this story to destroy, but just hear me out. You know you're the best at this, so why not go out with a bang? This OHM story will be the biggest that our firm has ever seen! Don't tell me that doesn't excite you?"

"I'm in a different head space now, than when I originally agreed to it, so no, this does not interest me anymore." Levi rubbed his forehead roughly, and his brows became wrinkled with irritation and frustration. "Like I said, let me get back to you on this. I'm busy right now."

"If I didn't know any better, I'd think you were sleeping with the chick," the woman teased and Jamaika turned completely to look at him for some sort of explanation. "Wait, let me guess, you're with her now?"

Levi ended the call quickly and tossed his phone to the loveseat. He was quiet for a moment and then nudged her.

"Sorry about that. Business call."

"I figured as much." Jamaika watched him under her thick, curly eyelashes until he returned her stare. "What was that about? She sounded demanding...and rude."

Levi rolled his eyes. "Or at least she tries to be. That was my assistant, and she was referring to

157

an old story I was supposed to complete. Since my promotion from Public Affairs Manager to the Public Relations Director, I pretty much gave away the biggest story of my career, and the salary increase that came along with it."

"Oh, wow. Why's that?"

"Priorities," he answered and shrugged, as though it were no big deal.

Who in their right mind would say no to a pay increase and positive recognition? As much as she wanted to mention more of what she had heard to him, she figured it was none of her business, and turned back to see what the families were doing on the game show.

Chapter Fourteen

"Thank you for calling Nelly's Deli, how may I help you?"

"Hi, yes, I'd like to place an order for pickup, please," Jamaika spoke openly in her truck.

The windows were down, and her sunroof was ajar. She had her hands-free Bluetooth setup, and could drive without distraction.

"Sure. What's your name?"

"Jamaika."

"Okay, Miss Jamaika. What would you like to order?"

She listed off about five things and received her total. She was nearly speeding to Levi's workplace, hoping to catch him while he was still on lunch. Although he was not expecting her, she was sure he would be happy to see her.

There was a deli adjacent to his office, and that would make it easy for Jamaika to pick up the food and then head right up. As promised, their food was ready within ten minutes, and she proceeded to the fourth floor elevators.

As the doors opened, she was met with the ample backside of a woman who was bent over in her file cabinets. Music played from the computer, and the phone rang constantly, so Jamaika was sure that her entrance had not been heard.

She cleared her throat so that she would not scare the young lady. "Excuse me."

The woman stood up quickly in surprise, adjusted her clothes, and then turned with an embarrassed but rehearsed smile.

"Yes? How may I help…you?"

Both women stopped in their tracks. The woman stumbled backward into her file cabinet, and Jamaika nearly dropped her Styrofoam boxes of food. Staring back at her with a nametag on, and looking much more professional than previous encounters, was Malia.

"First Lady…"

"It's just Jamaika," she quickly corrected her and looked unimpressed. "May I please speak with Mr. Daniels?"

Malia picked her jaw up from the floor finally and rounded her desk. She typed rapidly at her keyboard for a second, and then looked up nervously.

"I don't see your name anywhere on his schedule. Do you have an appointment?"

"I don't."

"Did you want to make one?" Malia suggested and it was apparent that she had no idea who she was talking to. "Is it regarding the article by chance?"

Jamaika waved a hand in dismissal, and her words slipped out quicker than she anticipated. "I normally don't have to make appointments to see my man."

Malia sat back completely and her drawn on eyebrows shot up in surprise.

"Wow, I didn't know you two were involved."

"There are a lot of things you probably don't know. You probably don't know that messing with another woman's husband is lowdown and classless. You probably don't know that you should *never* put on baby powder and wear black pants, and then bend over towards an entryway. Oh, and you

160

probably don't know that it was by the grace of God that I didn't rearrange your face all those times you pushed up on my husband. Need I say more, or do you get it?" Jamaika asked.

Malia continued to look shockeed and her words were stuffed at the back of her throat.

"Now, may I please see Mr. Daniels?" Jamaika repeated and she could not wait to tell Levi just what his assistant had been up to before her employment with his firm.

A now humbled and speechless Malia pointed a finger in the opposite direction. When she finally found her voice, it was filled with shame and remorse.

"Go ahead. He's in the executive conference room."

Jamaika headed down in the direction where Malia summoned her. Although she had never been to his office, she pretended to know where she going until she was sure she was out of view.

Her heart beat rapidly in her chest, and she willed the anger to go away. Jamaika was turning 34 this year, and she vowed that nothing or no one could bring her stress or steal her joy.

She closed in on a large room with voices coming from it. Glass windows surrounded the room so she peeked around to see if she could spot Levi. He was easy to find with his back turned to her. She could tell he was the big shot. He was the only one dressed casually with headphones draped around his shoulders, while all the other people wore business suits and professional attire. Plus, he was seated at the center of the rectangular table where other executives were.

They all watched a video, and near the end of it, someone stood up with a dry erase board. Another person wheeled over a projector.

"They still use those?" Jamaika pondered and leaned even more into the glass.

She kept quiet as she watched each executive stand and present Levi with a proposal. He either accepted or denied it, but was always respectful and attentive. A small smile tugged at her mouth. He looked so calm and sexy; he was so in control and passionate about what they were talking about.

Finally, after the last person spoke, he stood up and began talking, "Thank you all for your dedication to this project, and for your hard work with my transition. As you all are aware, I no longer want the OHM project because of personal reasons."

"You've never told us exactly why you backed out midway through this story, Mr. Daniels." A black woman with red lipstick and unattractively long fingernails spoke, "Did you want to share more with us today as we wrap things up?"

A balding, white man raised his hand this time.

"For starters, why don't you simplify your lingo a bit? Some of the execs via conference call may not understand which story you're referring to."

Levi nodded. "Fair enough. Well, to review, for the last year and a half, I have been heading the OHM project. It was slated for summer's release and is short for the Owens-Higgins-Ministry project."

The blood in Jamaika's face left completely. Her body froze, and her fingers lost any kind of

162

strength. The food that she had been holding fell to the carpet with a thud. As Levi continued talking, she felt her knees grow weak.

"Jalen Owens is a well-known pastor and community activist, with several businesses and lots of influence. Arlington Heights, Naperville, Lisle, and much of the Chicago area are aware of his scandals over the past few years, but no one has ever publicized them. He wants to run for mayor this fall, so his campaign is doing everything they can to cover up these scandals."

Levi pointed to a plaque at the front of the room. "Our firm is notorious at getting to the bottom of indignities, and rightfully revealing people who jeopardize the city's repute. I decided to take on this piece, which would publicize his adulterous and abusive relationship with his then wife, Jamaika."

A heavyset redhead spoke this time, and Jamaika recognized him as one of Jalen's former colleagues. They had worked on several construction ventures in the Oak Brook suburbs together until Jalen discontinued his contract.

"I've done business with the scumbag on a couple occasions and would agree that he's no hero. But why the sudden change? Why shouldn't we go public with this story, and expose him for the unlawful public figure he is?"

Levi looked to the screen where Jamaika's images flashed across it. It was the same photos that had nearly jeopardized her job and dignity. Tears were forming in her eyes by now.

"His ex-wife doesn't deserve the negative light it'll bring to her life and family. She has nothing to do with his wrongdoings, double life, and imperfections," Levi explained.

163

"But isn't it true that she was willing to sit with you and share her marital problems? Mind you, she was not divorced on the afternoon you two had coffee together," a male said.

His back was facing Jamaika so she could not see who was slandering her. The man continued, "She's no angel either, Mr. Daniels."

"You don't know her well enough to make that assumption."

The guy stood up from his seat and pointed a finger. "Neither do you!"

Levi stepped to the man who was challenging him and dared him to say another word. "Sit down. If there's a way to single him out, by all means do it, but I'm asking you to leave her out of it. That's final."

He was growing agitated by the second, and Jamaika's tear ducts were officially giving way. She wanted to believe that she was dreaming, but she was far from it, and the realization stung.

"Do you realize we'll lose out on a lot of revenue backtracking from your change of heart? You should have NEVER proposed a story of this magnitude if you knew you'd regret it! We had all kinds of people willing to come forward to share their experiences with Mr. Owens. We had sponsors supporting this project. This is so much greater than you and your feelings, Mr. Daniels."

Levi avoided the comments as he paced in front of the projector. His shadow danced across the wall as he walked.

"At the end of the day, this is now *my* department and *my* decision. I'm reneging because I refuse to hurt an innocent woman, all for the demise of a monster, and a nice paycheck."

"How are you hurting her? I'm confused."

"This would be hurting her because it would reopen the painful memories of what their relationship entailed. Their divorce is final, true, but she is still the victim in all of this. It would be hurtful to her because then the media would hound her and want to know more from her perspective. That's just not right. I would rather she move forward and heal without our company dragging her down in the process," Levi explained with sincerity in his voice.

To others, he may have looked delusional because he was fighting for someone he supposedly didn't even know, but half of the staff seemed to read between the lines. They knew it was more to this story.

"With that being said," he cleared his throat and continued, "any back prints of the story, get rid of them. Delete all of the digital copies and all pictures should be removed from all of the hard drives. There should be nothing archived. As far as Malia, she's cut all ties with Jalen and is helping to clean up this mess. Do I make myself clear? Do we understand what needs to be done?"

Levi wrapped up his meeting, and as the executives gathered their notepads and other belongings, he gave a final reminder, "Guys, I don't want any of this to get in Jamaika's hands. Trust me, she is not the villain here."

Jamaika stayed hidden from view as the room cleared. Everyone left except Levi and another man, who had kept quiet the entire meeting. A man, who she presumed was Levi's supervisor, finally stood up. He shook his head and placed his hand on Levi's shoulder.

He spoke in a fatherly manner, "You know I value your work here and I value your time at this company, but you did exactly what I said not to do.

Instead of piecing together the puzzle of this story, you got mesmerized and awe-struck with Jamaika and got in too deep. Now, look at this mess you've created."

"What do I do?" Levi dropped his head in his hands.

"You make it right." The man spoke with authority and walked away.

At that exact moment, Levi looked up and caught her saddened eyes through the glass. She was still pretty much frozen and stepping on food, and whatever else she had dropped. As he moved forward to catch up to her, she found the strength to take off running in the opposite direction. She pushed past men and women and went through several doors before slowing down.

Jamaika fell to her knees against a door and breathed in and out deeply. It all made sense now. Levi showing up in her life was all a part of a selfish master plan. Levi driving past while she and Jalen had dinner over Malia's house was strategic. Malia joining their ministry and getting in close with Jalen was all purposeful. Levi appearing in the coffee shop and in Fiji, begging for her to vent and trust him was not because he wanted to help her. It was all for *his* career and to make her look like an even bigger fool.

All of the sweet nothings he had whispered, and the home cooked meals were only done to keep her around. Levi only wanted her deepest secrets and miserable stories so he could write an article. He was one heck of a liar and Jamaika hated to admit it, but she had fallen for it all. How stupid of her.

Levi seemed to know exactly where she had stopped because he knocked once on the door,

166

before entering. Jamaika picked herself up from the floor and could not stop the blinding anger that overtook her. She pushed against his chest forcefully, and then pointed her fingernail into his chest with every word.

"I trusted you! I believed in you!"

"Baby, listen…"

"No, don't 'baby' me! I heard everything! You don't have to explain anything. All of this was a lie, Levi! How could you? You told me you loved me, and you LIED!"

She could no longer see clearly through her tears. He was much too strong for her and had stopped her erratic movements by holding onto her arms.

"Let me go!"

"No, I won't until you chill out and listen to me." Levi was so calm that it unnerved her.

"Chill out? How would you feel if you were in my shoes?" Jamaika attempted to yank herself free from his grip but he again, was much too strong. She looked down at her feet like an admonished child. "Let…me…go!"

"What are you doing here anyway? How did you find my workplace?" Levi questioned.

He was trying to change the subject, and she was not going to let this go.

"I was bringing lunch for a man I thought I had fallen in love with. I got your work address from your business card. Let me GO!" Jamaika screamed and kicked at his shin.

He doubled over in pain and that is when she broke loose. He limped to try to catch up to her, but she was reliving her high school track and field days and ran until she could run no more. Finally, she reached the private parking lot and sat in her truck for a second to catch her breath.

As she inhaled and exhaled, more and more tears fell and moistened her blouse. She was an emotional mess and knew one thing was for certain. Just as quickly as she had fallen for him, she wanted nothing to do with Leviticus Maurice Daniels.

Chapter Fifteen

A knock sounded at the window and even amongst thunder and rain, the taps were recognizable. The cadenced force behind it could only signify one person. Jamaika's heart thumped unsurely. She could be stubborn and ignore it, but her legs were already in motion, bringing her to stand before him. It was their first encounter since the office debacle.

Levi stood soaked in his clothes and shoes. It was a sight that she could not fully comprehend. Usually, he cared too much about his appearance to be caught in a full thunderstorm, let alone about to sabotage his health and new attire now. A single crucifix chain hung around his neck, glistening even in the dimness. She was grateful that lightning had not struck him.

"What are you doing here?"

Levi wore a cap backward on his head. There was nothing to shield his face from dampness. A stream of droplets became a river from the corner of his eye, curving along his jawline, and traveling past his lips to collect beyond his chin. Finally, the river of moisture soaked into the collar of his shirt. But then Jamaika squinted harder and saw that it was tears that were flowing. The rain had only kissed areas of his face.

"Hey." His voice was low as always and tonight she matched his mellowness, plus the weather helped none.

"Hi."

"Can I come in and talk to you?"

"About...?"

"You know what I want to talk about. Please, just…can I come in? It's raining."

"Like I don't see it." Jamaika gave him a long perusal before stepping backward. "I was in the middle of a movie, so you have ten minutes."

In reality, the movie had just gone off, and she was looking forward to a bath, but he could not know that. She wanted him in and out as soon as possible. She was embarrassed by the strong feelings she still had for him. This could not be healthy.

Levi pushed away from the doorframe and entered. He removed his cap from his head. He seemed too nervous about an invite to sit, so he remained standing and kept his head low as he bit his lip. She looked away, finding him incredibly attractive when he did that. She was such a weak idiot.

"How are you?"

"I'm fine."

He glanced up towards the staircase in thought. "How is…?"

"Look, you said you came to talk. I'm fine, my family's fine, but you're interrupting my movie. Either you start talking about what you came here to discuss, or I'll gladly show you the way out."

"I'm sorry," he mumbled. The sky-blue polo wrinkled at the shoulders as he shrugged. "The room feels so tense."

"Yeah, that's what happens when a friend betrays another friend."

"I didn't betray you, Jamaika. I didn't even know you when I decided to take on this project," Levi pleaded.

She sighed and decided to calm down some. There was no sense in getting worked up.

"Please, just talk. I don't want to waste either of our time."

"Right."

Levi dropped his head briefly into his open palms, and then glanced up to meet her distant eyes. Her entire demeanor had changed since he stepped into the house. Her spirit was now heavy with anguish and gloom. He had jeopardized much of her joy, and it pained him to know that.

"I think...no, I *know* that I made a mistake not being honest with you from the start."

Jamaika clapped her hands softly. There was sarcasm at the tip of her tongue but darn it, he looked so sorry and pathetic. She sat back on the plush loveseat and crossed her leg.

"While it was not my doing, I know it was all my fault that any of your pictures ended up in the newspaper. What started off as a good sales pitch, marketing strategy, and great idea, turned out to be one of my biggest regrets," Levi admitted and reached out for her, "I didn't expect to fall in love with you, and even if I hadn't. You still didn't deserve any of it."

"No, I didn't." She glanced down at her fingernails.

"I feel horrible, whether you believe me or not. There's really no excuse for what I did, but please know that I never meant to hurt you and I definitely didn't want you to find out that way." He was begging and it made her feel good that he felt so pitiful.

"As you know, my life since my mother's death has been a mess. I thought I had gotten myself together, then my world turned upside down with the passing of my wife..."

"And that gives you what right to hurt others?"

"It doesn't, but just let me finish. My joy was taken away. I've never felt TRULY happy after that and to this day, I'll never understand why so many people I loved were taken from me."

Levi threw his cap to the floor in frustration. "I will NEVER understand why I was the faithful husband who loved his family unconditionally, and would go to war for their happiness, but lost everything! I have to live with the memories of 'what if?' What if my baby girl had grown up to be as beautiful as her mother? What if my wife had never driven that night? What hurts most is that she was driving to pick ME up from the airport!"

Jamaika avoided his eyes but from her peripherals, she saw the tears form and his physical anxiety dictate his every move. Levi was literally trembling as he talked.

"So, imagine my irritation, running into your husband at that time. He talked about being this highly sought-after preacher and upcoming mogul. He bragged about this beautiful wife of his and the various women on the side. When my firm learned about his political campaign, I jumped on the opportunity to expose that ungrateful bastard. I felt like he deserved to burn in hell for the hypocrisy and greed I witnessed. My boss was game for whatever I had to do to get to the bottom of Jalen Owen's double life."

Levi punched the inside of his hand in excitement, and his mind seemed to travel back to sweeter memories.

"But you changed everything for me. I remember that day so well. As I entered that restaurant, you were walking over to the bar. I remember our entire exchange and thinking, you were nothing like your husband. I assumed you were just as money hungry and evil, but you were the complete opposite. I wanted to protect you right away because you were so vulnerable and innocent. You were literally the classiest, most beautiful woman I had ever seen. You still are," he spoke sincerely.

Jamaika stole a thorough peek at him. He looked so amused and in love as he described what she wore that day, and the way she accidentally injured him.

Levi was an exotic mix of African American and Korean parents. His complexion was the color of an espresso with vanilla creamer. His teeth were straight from two years of braces, and although his hair was low-cut, it was a rich, dark brown color. He was extremely easy on the eyes and even easier to love. Even now, her heart fluttered at his intense stare.

"I went home and called off everything. I told my boss to get rid of all of the pictures, and to pursue another person of interest. At that point, getting to know you was my ONLY focus. I sort of followed you everywhere," Levi laughed.

"I noticed," Jamaika said softly.

"I only had intentions of being a friend though. I didn't want to get between you and Jalen. I didn't want you to get in trouble for talking to me, but I liked you. Physically, you were stunning, but the more we talked, the more I realized how precious and different you were. My boss warned me to stay away from you, and to pick back up where I'd left off on the story. I couldn't do any of that though."

"So, what changed?" Jamaika asked as she finally looked him in the eye.

"I saw a bruise on your arm that day in the café. I wanted to snap, and when you opened up to me about Jalen's abuse and cheating, I knew I had to be that man for you. You were everything I wanted and needed in this messed up life of mine. You were...excuse me, *are* gorgeous inside and out, God-fearing, intelligent, compassionate, and gentle. What I admire most is that you're not confrontational, or cold-hearted despite what you've been through."

"And yet you still hurt me, knowing everything I did go through," Jamaika chuckled painfully and pointed out, "Are you hearing yourself right now? What if I took the pain from my past and hurt you out of anger for every person that did me wrong?"

"I know, I know, but..."

Jamaika stood up abruptly as she walked into the kitchen. She didn't really want to take the argument to the level she knew it could escalate.

"I'm getting tired, so you can begin to make your way out. I appreciate your explanations, but they mean nothing to me. *You* are nothing to me anymore."

Levi followed behind her and attempted to reach for her. "Whoa. Baby, don't..."

"No! Don't touch or 'baby' me because you had your chance to do that and more! I'm through, I'm tired, and I'm done with the surprises and the excuses. I forgive you, but an apology won't change what you did. I saw Sunday's paper, Levi. That whole little back and forth between you and your coworkers obviously didn't work. I saw the article. I read the headlines. I noticed the pictures. My name was dragged through the mud right along with Jalen's, and for what? I haven't done anything to anyone."

"I quit my job, Jamaika. I assumed they would let me out of this story, but when I came in the next day, my boss told me they were going forward with the information I had gathered. I tried so hard to stop them, but it was too late. So much money was invested, and my love for you didn't mean anything to them. I didn't mean to hurt you, I swear to God!"

"SO WHAT! You quit your job, because you assumed they would understand where you were coming from? So that's supposed to make me feel better? Let me get this right," Jamaika said sarcastically and put her index finger to her lips, as if in deep thought, "You let my ex-husband's actions shape what you thought of me and you ASSUMED that you had me all figured out. You ASSUMED that I was a bad person. When we got to know each other better, you should have told me the truth, but you ASSUMED that your company would understand and let you out of this project. I didn't ask for any of this. I was fine, moving forward with my life…"

"Listen to me."

She ignored his pleas. "But here I am, dealing with the aftermath of your ASSUMPTIONS that have hurt me in more ways than one. Your assumptions have been costly, Levi."

He succeeded in cornering her this time as she rounded the island counter. His hands held her upper arms to ensure that she was unable to move anywhere, and to make sure that she could look at his sincere expression.

But still, her voice softened above a whisper and her gaze failed to meet his. "Let me go."

"I can't." He placed his hand on her cheek in a tender caress. "I want to know if you really meant what you said earlier. I want to hear for myself that you no longer have feelings for me."

"Let me go...*now,*" she spoke firmly but lowly, and backed away from him to replay their history that seemed so perfect. "I won't deny my feelings for you, but that doesn't mean I'll continue to hang onto them. Since day one you were someone I wanted in my life. Maybe not romantically at first because your spirit was so lovable, and you gave me a great friendship to run to when things got chaotic. Then you just happened to steal my heart with your words and actions."

Jamaika hugged herself and smiled in remembrance.

"Oh, how your words gave me comfort and made me feel beautiful and special, unlike anything I had ever felt before. I wasn't the belittled First Lady, or the other woman. I was the woman who had a name, and you would say it so sweetly, so perfectly. I saved all of your text messages just to reread days later whenever I needed a reason to smile. We could have been powerful together but how silly of me to think there would be a fairytale ending, huh?"

Bitterness could be tasted on her tongue and pain was evident in her raspy voice.

"I decided to fall in love, to trust, and to give myself to someone again. It happened quickly, too. Reminder, Levi. I didn't want to be in a relationship and give my all for fear that something like this would happen. I stayed in prayer about your motives but you ended up being the epitome of my

176

dream man, so I took the chance because it was what my heart said and felt. That's not a good feeling, Levi."

"I didn't know I would fall in love…nor did I know my staff would go ahead and put the pictures in the article, or print the story."

"But you KNEW me, and you should have thrown everything away before that happened!"

By now, their voices were hoarse and strained; their faces were tainted with tears and harbored sadness.

"Do you not see the big picture? If you loved me, and if you were so interested in me like you claimed, why did you follow me, and still write about Jalen's relationship with me? Why did you give the story to Malia and allow her to enter our lives? You knew Jalen was attracted to her, and that would cause me more stress. Why, Levi? Why didn't you just tell me the truth before this all backfired? Why would you follow me to Fiji and still allow a reporter to photograph us?" Jamaika sighed at the fact that she appeared weak in front of him and turned to walk away. "I—I don't get it. Ugh…move."

She attempted to sidestep the arms that enclosed her, but it was impossible. She hit his chest with balled fists before allowing the tears to flow entirely. Her head involuntarily landed on his shoulder, and he placed his fingers through her hair, caressing her scalp and back.

"Baby, I'm sorry. I'm a man…I don't think about all of these things. Your love was still new to me, and I was blinded by what my job called me to do, versus what honesty should have led me to do."

For the first time, she was seeing him from the inside out. He was a little boy who had become this confused and pained shell of a man. Stripped from his comedic and suave personality, Levi was in rare form. She appreciated the baby steps he had taken to express his regret to her. Still, none of his confessions made any of this right.

If there was one thing that she learned between Jalen and Levi, it was that her heart and happiness was not to be played with. She could no longer set herself up for heartache and vowed never to allow another man to strip her of her happiness.

Jamaika wrapped her arm around him a final time, and then tapped his lower back to get his attention. "Hey."

"Yes." His voice was just above a whisper.

Jamaika nodded to the door and then stepped backward. "Your ten minutes are up. Have a good night."

Levi looked baffled, but words never left his mouth. He nodded and backed away slowly towards the living room and further away from their history. This was a goodbye and she was confident that it was long overdue. She should have followed her heart from the jump and allowed herself to be healed and renewed, without the distraction of another man hindering her process. Instead, she had done things on her own and look where it landed her…*broken*, once again.

Jamaika dropped her face in her hands. Her heart ached more than ever, and her clothes were now fragranced with his cologne. This meant she would smell him all night. Through shaky fingers, she watched the door swing closed softly and Levi's silhouette disappear gradually into the stormy night.

She screamed out in frustration and attempted to bury herself deep within the cushions so she wouldn't have to face the world so soon.

Levi's visit was needed to clear up her curiosities, but she felt even more upset. She had begun to move on with her life, but he had come back and resurfaced all of the memories that she thought were tucked safely away.

Her bath wasn't enjoyable, although it was bubbly and warm, and her sleep was interrupted and deprived. She had said it once, and she had said it twice, but the third time was a charm. She had to make a *major* change.

Chapter Sixteen

"So, you're really leaving me? After everything we've been through, you want to throw in the towel. Over what—some no-good men?"

Nadia stood with dejection written all over her face, while clutching a piping hot flat iron in her hands. With each word, her voice grew louder and louder.

Jamaika sighed hard.

"I love you. I do. It's not that I don't cherish this friendship, and you know I would never throw away what we had. It's just that I need to get away, girl. I'm no good for anyone right now."

In her hand, she clutched the silver friendship ring that Nadia had spent her hard-earned money on, when they were just teenagers.

"They say if you love something let it go, and if it comes back, then it's meant to be. I'm taking a leap of faith, sis. If Arlington Heights is where I should be, then I will return. And if not, it'll always have a special place in my heart. You know I got you, and we'll always keep in touch."

Nadia had approached her at their high school freshman orientation, asking if she wanted to be in her icebreaker group. For months and even years later, the two were inseparable until their college graduation. Nadia was whisked away by an older sibling to New York to pursue her graduate career. Jamaika stayed in Illinois, where she met and fell in love with Jalen.

He was a drummer at a local church and worked for the neighborhood food market, and after their initial meeting, they became good friends. Months down the line and after running into each other by chance at a mutual friend's wedding, Jalen ended up with the keys to her heart and the bragging rights of being her first kiss. They married quickly and became one, and she soon found herself without an identity.

She stood now, wanting that piece of herself back. She had given away too much, to people who did not deserve her and wanted the old Jamaika. She wanted the woman *before* marriage, *before* the abuse, *before* the scandals, and *before* the unhealthy friendships and relationships that came with dealing with Jalen.

Nadia inched closer until she could hug her friend tightly.

"This isn't even possible right now. You are my girl, you hear me? We're supposed to be going to Italy in five months, and you're leaving? Jamaika, please, don't do this."

Nadia was beginning to get worked up all over again and had so many questions. Jamaika wished that she had all of the answers. She heard the slight crack in her friend's usually mellow voice and turned from her; she would be unable to deal if she saw tears.

Literally 12 hours before, she had awakened in a cold sweat with an epiphany so strong that she now had a large duffel bag packed in her car. No matter how much it hurt, this getaway was necessary for growth, healing, and confirmation of the next steps in her life. Warm tears cascaded down her skin and she mirrored Nadia's sorrow while she quickly wiped her eyes.

"Jay, please. We can make it through whatever you're dealing with. I promise. Forget Jalen, and forget Levi…"

No words could soothe her heart, nor could any words change her mind. She had to get away—far, far away.

"Nadia, I will explain later, and I will come back for you then," Jamaika promised.

It was like a movie scene where two lovers parted forever. It felt like she was leaving her friend eternally, but really it was only temporary. She just needed time and space to get her broken heart together. Jamaika wiggled free from her friend's embrace and kissed her cheek.

"For now, you have to trust me and release me. Goodbye, Nadia."

Without another look back, Jamaika turned and exited the break room, and left out of the side of the boutique that Nadia co-owned. Yells and footsteps followed Jamaika halfway down the busy block, but she was on a mission and had no time to stop. She shoved a pair of chocolate-colored shades onto the bridge of her nose. They shielded her eyes from the sun and hid the tears from onlookers. The taps of her heels echoed off of the alleyway as she scurried from her past.

Inside her truck she settled and barely started up the engine before she sped off, tire skids and all. The air conditioning was likely needed for a day like this, but she wanted to experience God's peace and beautifully crafted weather.

Jamaika rolled all of the windows down so that the wind could blow in. The summer heat was no joke today, and as the weatherman had predicted, temperatures were pushing high 90s with a touch of humidity that made every black girl frown. With not a fear that her hair would be ruined, Jamaika slid her hands through her much shorter do. Her hair was chopped purposely and dyed creatively. Nadia told her best beautician to hook her up the moment she sauntered in, and although Jamaika loved long hair on her head, she was proud of what only a relaxer and sharp shears could do.

The flimsy dress she wore fell to reveal her collarbone and shoulder that was newly tattooed with a cherry blossom down her entire right side. The blossom symbolized seasons and change. Change had definitely crept into her life, and her hair had to go. New art was inked on her forever. She felt new, she felt free.

Her eyes made the mistake of looking back where she saw a set of car seats, both new and unused. One was pink and the other was blue. They had been in her basement for over two years, and she knew soon enough she would have to give them away to someone who could actually put them to use.

Her foot mashed the gas as she maneuvered through the downtown area, and well into Southern Illinois. Where she was going, she did not know, but she had to get some miles behind her.

A soft smile touched her lips. She thought back to everyone she had left behind. Days ago, she enjoyed a nice dinner with her family, and they parted on good terms. Despite their more recent troubles, she could count on their support whenever she made it back into town. While she hated to leave them hanging, it was needed for her growth. Plus, healing needed to take place in their lives respectively. She had to experience life without her "crutches" and had to be freed from the frustrations from her childhood. Jamaika knew that with time, all would be well.

To her surprise, but with Divine Intervention assuring her, the unthinkable happened just the other day. As she thought about that moment, Jamaika swallowed hard and her eyes narrowed with moisture.

"Uh, Ms. Higgins? You have a visitor. It's urgent. Shall I send him in?"

Jamaika attempted to look through the blinds and out of the window. She could not decipher who was standing in front of her receptionist's desk, but knew it was, for sure, a gentleman.

"Hmmm. Okay, does he want to make an appointment? What is he here for? I was leaving shortly."

Ivanna lowered her voice into the receiver, "It's your ex-husband…and he's crying."

Jamaika swallowed hard and okayed him to enter. She had no idea why Jalen was at her workplace or why he was overcome with emotion, but she watched him enter into her office and fall to his knees immediately.

"What's going on, Jay?" she asked, jumping to her feet in alarm. She wasn't sure if she should have Ivanna page security or not.

He looked like he had been up all night. There was a hint of remorse on his face, and he seemed sincere when he began to speak.

"I have NOTHING! I messed up. I ruined what we had. I took our love for granted and look at us now!"

"Yeah, look at us now," she repeated, unaffected. "I know now that the newspaper article wasn't your fault, but Jay, why are you here?"

"I'm here to apologize. I'm here to say I want you back. My daughters' mother is CRAZY. She doesn't do half the stuff you do, and she stole some of the church earnings. I realize how special you are; I realize that you didn't deserve anything that I put you through. I realize how much I need and LOVE you!"

184

Jamaika held up her hand and stood from her desk. She walked around in her bare feet because her shoes had been kicked off.

She spoke firmly, "That's all too late, Jalen. I understand you regret some things, but I'm done. You thought it was best for you to do your dirt and have your fun outside of our marriage. You thought it was the right choice to divorce me and leave me for another woman. That's fine. Now, I have to do what's best for ME, and it's not you."

"Baby, please don't...don't do this. God has changed me! He's given me a new mindset and focus." He pressed his tear-stained face to the side of her leg.

"I'm happy for you. That's awesome that God has changed some things in your life, but I can't be with you. I'm sorry. I have moved on, and if you loved me like you say you do, then you'll let me go."

Jalen was silent as he continued to weep. This was so unlike him to be so vulnerable, so transparent. He never showed emotions, especially when it put him in a position of rejection. That's the only way she knew that he was changed but still, it wasn't enough. It was much too late. The damage had been done.

"I dedicated almost half of my life to you. I cannot do it any longer, honey," Jamaika said and walked over to the door. "I forgive you, now please leave."

Jamaika appreciated his efforts and change of heart, but their time and season was over. As she thought about that moment, she swallowed hard and her eyes narrowed with moisture. Of all the men, Jalen had hurt her most. He had ruined her innocence and perception of marriage and loyalty; he had introduced imaginable heartache and pain to her life.

They were best friends and committed spouses at one point, and she could remember when she felt safe with him, but his mind no longer matched hers one day, and his speech no longer spoke of respectful, kind things. She became the victim of sexual, mental, and physical torture and to this day, she still had the scars to prove it. But God had changed him, and as she said goodbye, all was forgiven and that was enough.

Lastly, there was Levi. With a single text message, she told him that she was leaving and that she hoped he had learned his lesson. Tears welled up in her eyes, but this time it was with joy for what was to come. She had so much to look forward to. There was no family waiting for her, nor was there a six-figure job that she needed to jump into, but for the time being, there was a freedom that needed to be exercised, and that was the liberty from her past and the guys who had entered and impacted it somehow. She held her head high already, but even more so now that her secrets were confessed before the Lord.

She did not need to depend on any man, except the One who had created Heaven and Earth.

For hours, she drove and sang. For hours, she meditated and prayed. For hours, she worshipped and talked to herself. Contentment rested in her eyes as she looked towards a beach and drove along its coast. It looked deserted but proved to be the perfect stop to stretch and walk around a bit.

Jamaika exited her truck and grabbed two items from the backseat. Slowly, she walked towards the clear-bluish waters of Serene Beach. "What a perfect name," she admired.

Her eyes closed against the gentle wind and she inhaled deeply to smell the saltiness of the surrounding air. She kicked off her shoes one by one and stepped in the water. The warmth of the ripples tickled her toes. She could not believe how empty the beach was, but she could appreciate her alone time and thanked the Lord for it.

Jamaika sat there for hours. She drew pictures with sticks, built sandcastles, splashed water between her hands, and just enjoyed her moment and her time. Oftentimes she kept busy and never stopped to just breathe and enjoy the moment. She always wanted to please and do right by others and yet she had lost herself in the process, but she was determined to put an end to that and return home different.

"Well, I think it's time I head out, and continue on. But before I go." She pulled two sheets of paper from her purse. "I want to say goodbye for now."

Jamaika placed her unborn son's ultrasound in what should have been his car seat, and then she sat her unborn daughter's image in the pink one.

"Mommy will see you again someday."

She blinked slowly to control her emotions and took in the picture of twin car seats facing the gorgeous beachside view. She turned her back reluctantly, with a smile, "Bye, babies. I love you."

Her arms wrapped around her body, and her mind drifted elsewhere for a moment. She remembered from years ago how cold the stirrups were as doctors probed her lower stomach and told her that she had suffered a miscarriage.

Months later, she collapsed after a jog, and found herself in the same position, but somehow pregnant again. Her previous miscarriage had only been one of two children, and a baby boy now grew gradually inside of her. For three full weeks she enjoyed him; she enjoyed the way he shivered inside of her. She loved feeling his slight movements and late night stirring. She deeply missed his warmth and his sweet and perfect love.

But one day, things felt different. Motherhood was taken from her, and she was again, without a child. Twin-to-Twin Transfusion Syndrome was the name of the condition. It was unknown to her, but it had claimed the lives of both of her miracle babies.

Painfully, she remembered how she handled much of it all alone. Jalen was out doing his thing and had not bothered to question her well-being. Jamaika told no one, not even her parents. The depression and sadness she felt would not leave no matter how hard she tried. She thanked God to this day for giving her twins anyhow, because it was double the love and the blessings.

On the other hand, losing her children was an indication that God was still in control. It showed her that the season and timing was far from right. She would have hated to reproduce with Jalen. Whenever God blessed her with another husband, she knew He would bless her with children again as well.

Finally, Jamaika returned to her car, dusted off her feet, and rode off into the setting sun. She only looked in the rearview once and it was to offer a goodbye to the heartache, the sleeping pills, the disappointments, and the unexplainable anger.

She was bidding a goodbye to the restless nights, and the act of pretending like things were okay when they were far from. She was saying goodbye to the lies and infidelity of her exes, along with the stresses of her current line of work. Most importantly, she was offering a goodbye to the past. God promised in Revelations that He would make all things new, and until then, she needed to get away.

"Charlotte, here I come," she whispered.

Chapter Seventeen

Jamaika arrived at her hotel in downtown Charlotte, almost a day later. She literally drove until she could drive no longer, pulled over to rest, and then continued her trek when she had the energy. She made purposeful stops to different landmarks, ate good food, and took lots of pictures. Before long, she ended up at one of the most stunning hotels she had ever seen, and in one of her favorite cities based on the southern hospitality alone.

She had previously text her hotel information to Nadia and her parents, just to be on the safe side, and then turned off her phone completely while she drove. She sent another text to let them all know that she had arrived, and then again, turned off her phone. Jamaika had a chunk of cash in her backpack, and some of her most important necessities. She hoped that was all she needed because it was too late to turn back now.

She checked into her room and began the long journey up to the sixteenth floor. The staff was friendly and welcoming. Her stomach growled softly as she passed by the in-house restaurants and enjoyed the yummy aromas. Even the elevators were upscale and designed with prestige. Jamaika was glad that a coworker had suggested this getaway. She was going to enjoy every moment and bask in her time away from work and all other obligations.

Jamaika finally neared her room and was shocked to find that the door was slightly ajar. She knocked a few times before entering and expected a room attendant to be finishing up. What she did *not* expect was the long, athletic body lying on her bed, with his back facing her. She knew immediately the body belonged to Levi, and he was sound asleep. His deep breathing echoed off of the spacious walls of the suite. His luggage was thrown to the floor, and he was just as tired as she was, since he still wore his shoes in the bed.

"You've got to be kidding me," Jamaika said and dropped her duffel bag.

She walked closer and thought about calling hotel security. Then she contemplated calling the police. Lastly, she figured she should call Nadia to ask why she had given him the details of her whereabouts. But Jamaika did none of that. Levi had made it to her room before she did, so he must have flown to beat her there.

She was not sure if this was some cruel joke, or a way to win her back, but she was upset. "Levi!" Jamaika's voice was gentler than she wanted it to be, and he remained snoring with not a care in the world.

As she leaned to shake him awake, her headache began to grow by the minute. Her relaxed state was ruined, and he was causing her to become physically ill the more she stood there, attempting to wake him. Finally, she balled her fist and slammed it into his shoulder. She remembered he said he had a dislocated shoulder that never seemed to heal from playing semi-pro football.

He awakened with a groan and grabbed his shoulder. "Ow! What did you do that for?"

"What are you doing here? How did you know I was here in the first place?" Jamaika backed away as he reached for her. "Get OUT before I call the police on you!"

"Hold up, babe," he spoke sleepily and blinked to clear his eyes.

She was not sure how long he had been asleep, but he had bags beneath his eyes, and wrinkles along his normally smooth skin. She hoped that he had suffered, cried, and lost sleep just as much as she had. Many nights, she would pray that prayer of vengeance.

"Why did you leave me?"

"Leave you?" Jamaika questioned and began gathering her bags. He rushed to regain his footing and followed behind her. "I don't have to answer to you. You are NOT my man or my father!"

Levi fell to the floor and she looked back. A piece of her was concerned that he had hurt himself, and the other part of her wanted to smile that he had tripped. "What are you doing? Get up, and get out!"

"Not without you, Jamaika."

In his unstable hands was a small box that he extended towards her. She noticed the sparkle of the diamond and the glisten of the sterling silver band before he even took it out of its encasing.

"I know I messed up. I know I hurt you. But I also know that you're the one for me and if I have to spend a lifetime proving that, then so be it. Please forgive me and marry me, Jamaika."

She had no idea what to say and could not articulate an appropriate response. For a long while, she turned with her back facing him and hung her head. He remained kneeling and she could feel his eyes burning a hole through her back. She could feel his desperation and sincerity, and honest to God, she believed that he was sorry. To be honest, she had long ago forgiven him, but she just needed time. She needed space. Why was that so hard for everyone to understand?

"Please leave."

"Not without you, Jay, and not until you answer my question."

"Do you want me to call down to the front desk? Because I will," she threatened. She headed towards the door again. Jamaika crossed her arms. "LEAVE!"

A girl, who was no older than 11 or 12, was passing by the room and looked in. She screamed in possibly the highest octave that Jamaika had ever heard.

"Ooooh, my stars! You're the woman on the poster!"

Jamaika looked back at her. "What poster? I think you have me confused with someone else."

"No, no." She looked down the hallway and grinned. The metallic wire of her braces gleamed. "Mom, this is the woman on the billboard we saw!"

"Honey, what are you referring to? I'm just a tourist. I highly doubt you saw my face on a..."

Jamaika looked back at the window where the preteen pointed. It was her first time seeing the billboard since entering the room. She had been so distracted with Levi that it went unnoticed previously.

One of her favorite photographs of she and Levi was plastered on a billboard that overlooked downtown Charlotte. It was a selfie they had taken one night, while dining in a jazz club. They both were glowing like a young couple in love, and not a care in the world. Levi's arms were wrapped around her as she leaned into him, and he was kissing her cheek while she faced the camera. One of the biggest, happiest smiles was on her face. The billboard was positioned perfectly above her hotel room, and across the bottom there was a message.

I screwed up. I wasn't thinking. That's why I need you, your love, and your brain. Marry me?

Jamaika walked closer to the window. She stared at their image in awe. She suppressed a smile at the corny message and looked back at him.

"I cannot believe you tracked down my whereabouts and traveled this far, rented a billboard space, and even bought an engagement ring. Why?"

"I have to make this right, baby."

"What is it about me? Why do you love me so much?"

"What is there *not* to love about you?" Levi questioned.

As cool as he normally was, it was refreshing to see him still begging and leaning on one knee.

"I'm not trying to be a hero. I'm not trying to be your superman. I just want to be the man that catches your tears and tells you it's okay. I want to be the man to raise healthy children with you, and to provide them with all the joys I never had growing up. I just want to be there, every day that you wake, to tell you how beautiful you are."

Jamaika was silent. She had her hands cupped around her face in shock. They had a little audience out in the hall by now, and Jalen's eyes seemed to pierce through her soul.

"Baby…Queen…" Levi licked his lips and spoke up louder, "Jamaika Mercedes Higgins, will you marry me?"

A piece of her wanted to say yes, but the bigger part of her had another answer in mind. She closed her eyes and shook her head. "No. I—I can't. I'm sorry, Levi. I can't marry you."

Levi's face and demeanor dropped. His expression went from hopeful to dejected and the few people outside of their room, being nosey, took that as their cue to leave. She could not marry this man, not so soon and not under these circumstances. He had to learn that he could not always get his way.

"I guess I'll just go," he summed up with defeat in his voice.

"Maybe you should. Thank you for this though."

Levi gathered his bags and looked like he was deep in thought. "I'll drive back home in the morning. It was worth a shot. No matter what, I still love you."

She ignored the way her heart skipped a beat at his professions. "Where are you staying for tonight?"

"I'll see if they have another room available." Levi kept his eyes low and then nodded his departure. "Take care, love."

"See you."

Jamaika knew she was probably in the wrong. After all, most women would have taken him back for his efforts and sincere actions. But unlike her mistakes in the past, she knew there were a few things that she had to get out of the way before committing to anything and anyone else.

When she was alone again, she kneeled down and began to pray with her hands clasped.

"God, I know I've jumped the gun with a lot of things. I realize that I did not go to you before marrying Jalen, and I did not go to you before dating Levi. Both relationships have ended in

195

disaster, but I have to know, God. I have to know if he is the one," Jamaika pleaded. "Please confirm and reveal to me if Levi is my future husband. I don't want to make any more mistakes. I don't want to have my heart broken anymore. I don't want to stray further from Your Will because of any man or distraction. In Jesus's name, I pray. Amen."

She decided to freshen up and then go down to one of the restaurants. She dressed formally in a royal blue jumpsuit and curled her hair. If there was one thing that she had to learn being single, it was to be independent and treat herself from time to time. That is what the trip was about. She had to do things on her own now.

The restaurant was upscale and hardly anyone filled its booths or stools. She requested a small table near the back of the restaurant and ordered a virgin strawberry daiquiri, a platter of chicken nachos, and a fudge brownie for dessert.

Her waiter brought out all of her food at the same time as she asked, and then apologized.

"I will be getting off early because of a family emergency, but another server will be taking care of you. His name is Jaylin and if you need anything, he can assist you. It was my pleasure serving you, ma'am."

Jamaika paused as she was biting into a nacho loaded with chicken and Pico de Gallo. Had she heard what she thought she heard? Was his name really Jaylin or was she hearing things?

Sure enough, as she reached into her wallet to prepare for the check, the next waiter came out and was named Jaylin. He smiled politely and tapped his fingers against her table to catch her attention.

"I love your eyes," he complimented.

"Thank you." She smiled in return.

"May I ask who you're here with? I know an attractive woman like you has to have a date."

"Oh, I have a date. January 25th. That was my birthday this year," Jamaika challenged him and slid her credit card in his booklet. "Now what?"

"That's a good one." The waiter chuckled and tucked his booklet into the front pocket of his apron. "I'm sorry I bothered you."

"You didn't bother me. I just have a lot on my mind."

He nodded. "Understandable. Well, I'm here if you need anything. I do mean anything."

She ignored the emphasis he put on his words and thanked him for his service. He promised to return with her receipt. Then a woman that was shrieking with gladness caught her attention. She held up her left hand and admired a stunning diamond ring that was nestled there. Apparently, she had just been proposed to, and her face held an indescribable glow. Jamaika smiled and thought about how happy the woman must have felt.

As she gathered her belongings and shrugged on her wrap, she saw another couple seated further down from her. They were older and holding hands while they shared an ice cream sundae. The two had to have been pushing their late eighties or early nineties and yet their love was timeless.

"Alright. Here is your copy. You can sign whenever you're ready," Jaylin announced. "Now, are you sure you're fine?"

"I'm okay. Thanks for asking," she said shortly. "Have a good day."

"I know it's none of my business," he continued and lowered his voice so that only she could hear it, "But you've stared at all these couples. You go from smiling to frowning. Either you hate to see people happy, or someone has your mind all in shambles."

"Excuse me?"

"Am I right? Did someone, let's say a spouse, hurt you recently? Are you holding onto a grudge that you need to let go?"

"Excuse…me?" She repeated her words and looked at him like he was growing another head on his shoulders.

"I ain't no preacher, but the Bible says, 'Do not seek revenge or bear a grudge against anyone among your people, but love your neighbor as yourself.' That's Leviticus 19:18, to be exact," the waiter continued.

Jamaika began to choke. She felt like she was a part of a prank. Not only was her waiter named Jaylin, but now he was trying to minister to her with scriptures out of the book of Leviticus. God had to have done this on purpose. His sense of humor was uncanny, and she could not help but to laugh.

"If that's not confirmation, I don't know what is," Jamaika mumbled to herself. She planned to settle in her bed and relax well into the next morning.

What a day, what a day.

Chapter Eighteen

Jamaika stayed in North Carolina for over a week before she got an unexpected call to return home because it was an emergency. Her father was clinging to life after a freak accident during his annual hunting trip with his brothers. He had been shot twice—once in his lower spine and in his temple. Miraculously, he had stayed conscious enough to call 911, before blacking out. He had been declared paralyzed and brain dead, with very little chances of survival.

Jamaika could not remember ever driving so speedily and had to have covered ten hours of driving in just under six. Thankfully, no highway patrol officers had stopped her or her lead foot along the way.

She prayed, worshipped, cried, and prayed some more as she drove. According to her mother and brother, he was unable to speak and had been in a comatose state since his arrival to the hospital. It was like a nightmare that she was living, and she blamed herself for taking her little "Eat, Pray, Love" trip at a time like this.

"I'm so sorry this happened to you, Daddy. Please hang in there," she whispered to no one in particular.

When she made it to the hospital, it was well after nine in the morning. Her eyes were bloodshot, her skin was pale, and her fingernails were all bitten off and jagged. Concern was etched on her face as she sought direction from the receptionist and then scurried to the room that was assigned to her father.

"Baby, you've made it!" Her mother turned and greeted her with a weak smile.

Jamaika fell into her mother's arms and allowed the tears to escape. They wept together and hugged for another minute or so. Only when Jamaika began to talk did they finally break away.

"How's he doing? Has there been any progress?"

"He still hasn't responded to any of our voices or touches. The doctor said he has a very weak pulse, and he is unable to breathe on his own," her mother explained. "I have prayed, and I have asked God to heal his body. Other than that, I don't know what to do!"

"Shhh. It's okay."

"I feel so helpless! I shouldn't have let him go on that hunting trip!"

"Don't torture yourself with that kind of thinking, Momma." Jamaika kissed her mother's cheek. "All we can do is trust God. Here, sit down. Have you eaten?"

"I have no appetite, baby, but I'll try to put something in my stomach today," her mother admitted and shook her head. "How was your trip? Did you get what you needed out of it?"

"It was going amazing until I got the call. I feel so helpless and guilty because I could not be here for y'all."

"Now it's my time to encourage you. Don't blame or beat yourself up over it. You made it here faster than I expected. Plus, whether he's conscious or not, your father knows you love him dearly."

Jamaika shook her head with fresh tears on their way out of her eyes. "This is so surreal with him lying there and those tubes hanging in and out of his body."

"I know, baby, but your father is strong. God will see Him through this. I am positive."

"Amen."

"I know you must be beat, Punkin. Relax."

Jamaika settled on a corduroy couch in the corner of the hospital room the same time that the door opened. She looked up and assumed it was one of the nurses checking in on her father, but it was someone she never expected to run into so soon, and especially at a time like this.

Levi stood in the doorway with a single white rose and a grey tray of steaming, hot food. He wore a solemn expression on his face as his eyes landed on her father's slumped body. He did not notice Jamaika right away, and made a beeline for her mother where they hugged like old friends. Jamaika watched as her mother patted his back and thanked him for coming.

"Of course. When I got your phone call, I tried to make it down as quickly as possible," he explained and then handed her the rose. "Have you eaten? I stopped by the food court and picked you up something just in case."

"You're so sweet, honey. Thank you."

Jamaika watched in confusion as her mother, whom she thought had never met Levi, turned to her with a smile.

"Oh! Meet my daughter. Levi, this is my daughter, Jamaika. Punkin, this is Leviticus."

"Why are you here?" Jamaika questioned.

"Don't be rude, chil'. He was the young man jogging close to where your father was shot. He called the ambulance and kept him from bleeding too badly by applying pressure to the wound."

Levi's smile faded. He extended his arm and approached her with caution. In his eyes was affliction; he pretended not to know her. "Nice to meet…"

"Hey, Levi," Jamaika said dryly and cut him off. "Momma, we already know each other."

"What? It's a small world. How so?" Her mother looked back and forth between them with a smile.

"Long story," Jamaika said and hugged Levi.

There was no way that she could explain to her mother that this was the man she had fallen in love with in just a short time after divorcing her devil of a husband. There was no chance on earth that she would tell her mother that Levi had proposed to her and she had rejected him. In her mother's eyes, he was a hero, so she chose to leave their history out…for now.

"But thank you for helping to save my father. That means a lot to us, and for him, too."

"It was my pleasure." He clapped his hands, looked back at her father, and then turned back around. "Well, I'll let you two spend some time with Mr. Nelson. Please let me know if you need anything. I'll be praying for you all."

"Levi, wait." Jamaika held her hand up to keep him from leaving. "Momma, can I speak with him for a moment? Call or text me if Daddy moves or anything."

"Will do. Thanks for the food, again, sweetheart!"

The two walked in awkward silence towards the elevator. There, they boarded an empty elevator and stood across from each other. Levi kept his gaze on her while she avoided his eyes and watched the red numbers grow lower and lower.

Finally, she said the one thing that came to mind. "You know, since you left, there has been this empty place in my heart. I cannot explain it; I cannot describe it, but it hurts that we were not communicating. I know it was my fault, but I was sad to see you go that night."

Levi remained quiet.

"I prayed for you. I prayed the second you left my hotel room that God would reveal some things to me. As deeply rooted in Christ as I have been my entire life, I never went to God about my ex-husband. I never went to God about you either. So naturally, I was terrified that whatever decision I made next would result in failure. I could not accept that marriage proposal no matter how much I cared for you, and I hope you understand that now."

He nodded and seemed to comprehend what she was trying to articulate. He continued to watch her until they came to the bottom level. He put his arm out so that she could exit the elevator first.

"The ring was beautiful. Your gesture was beautiful. The billboard greeted me every morning that I spent in Charlotte and was a constant reminder of how much I missed and loved you," Jamaika continued as they found two empty, adjacent seats. "I wanted to call you every day. I wanted to reach out and see how you were doing, but I was always taught to learn to love God and myself *first*, and then offer up my love to another *after*."

He cautiously reached out to hold her hand. "What are you saying?"

"I'm saying that with Jalen, there was no self-love or self-respect. My relationship with God was severed and I pretty much ran to the first man who showed me affection. I was young when we got together and I knew nothing about marriage, myself, what true love was, how to be a wife, none of that. Overtime, I learned, but my perception of true love was way off. I grew up in a household where the women carried the weight, stayed in the kitchen, and the men sat back and did 'manly things.' So, when I was introduced to a husband who took away my voice and authority, I pretty much self-destructed. Add abuse and infidelity into the equation, and I, as you know, was ready to take my own life."

Levi held her hand up to his lips and kissed it gently.

"Fast forward to meeting you. Baby, you were everything I dreamed of. You embodied EVERYTHING that most women desire in a husband and companion, and I truly believe you're a man after God's own heart. Your intentions were pure. You were only doing your job. I get that. By then, I was still getting to know and love myself, so it was hard for me to push aside your small mistakes and see the bigger picture. This trip taught me all of that. God healed and rewired my heart in a matter of DAYS, and I can honestly say I would love to be your wife. There's no other thought or person that comes to mind when I wake up and when I fall asleep. I swear to you, Levi, I asked for confirmation from God and He's shown me your face every…single…day. He's given me some sort of sign every…single…day."

He continued to listen beside her, but the corners of his mouth had now lifted. She could feel the weight leave his shoulders. Clearly, he was relieved to hear her professed love.

"My final wakeup call about you was the fact that God placed you in the right place at the right time to help save my father. If that wasn't God slapping me over the head to get my attention, then I don't know what was."

They both laughed for a moment. Jamaika sat back in her seat and crossed her leg. She admired the side of his face. He dropped his head briefly, and there was a single tear that fell from his eye and onto his pant leg.

"Man! You don't know how amazing that feels to hear you say that. I thought I lost you forever, so imagine my surprise to run into you here. What's even more amazing is your mother had no idea about us, but she mentioned that she 'had a beautiful, very single daughter who wears a size 12 and has no kids,'" Levi chuckled.

"Oh, my goodness! She did NOT give you my size and SAY ALL OF THAT! You've got to excuse her." Jamaika pressed her palm into her forehead.

"No, no. I was flattered that she even thought of me in that way. She's a sweetheart…just like you."

Jamaika reached out and placed her hand on his knee. "Will you forgive me for pushing you away?"

"Only if you agree to be my wife. I can't do life with you."

"I love you, Levi," Jamaika whispered and pressed her forehead to his. "Yes, I will marry you."

"I love you too, Jamaika. May I?" He rubbed his thumb over her naturally pouty lips. "May I kiss you?"

"*Please*," she begged softly and closed her eyes.

As they shared a short-lived but affirming kiss, a vibration could be felt below her waistline. It was her phone ringing in her pocket. Her mother's picture danced across the screen.

"Yes, Momma? Any good news?"

"Your father opened his eyes! It's a MIRACLE! Come to the room now!"

Jamaika never ran so quickly in her life. As she rounded the corner to get to the room, with Levi in tow, she planned to tell her parents everything. As ironic as their destiny had been, she knew her father would not have a problem with her and Levi becoming engaged without his blessing. She was happy to have her family back stronger than ever, and her father still alive and well with her man by her side.

Epilogue

Six-inch heels slapped the concrete rhythmically, loudly, and downright unapologetically.

Freshly relaxed tresses swayed gently in the early autumn breeze; it was a hairstyle fresh out of the magazines. Puckered, glossy lips rubbed together in confidence, and only opened to stretch the mint-flavored gum in a bubble. She wore new clothes and shoes to complement her new walk and talk. No one could tell Jamaika anything, especially since it was her 39th birthday.

The double-breasted fuchsia pea coat that her husband had gifted her was fastened more tightly to eliminate the brisk winds from slapping at her stocking-clad thighs. Her eyes looked around quickly before she crossed the street to her truck. She started it up and the CD picked up where she had left off hours before.

As she turned it to a comfortable volume, she smiled at the befitting song. The Clark Sisters' "Blessed & Highly Favored" played, and she sung the lyrics that could not have been more appropriate.

Five green lights later and Jamaika was parked out front of a three-story lakefront home. Simultaneously, her smartphone vibrated inside of her clutch. Already knowing the caller, she spoke quickly into the plum-colored device before getting out.

"Hey, I just pulled up."

A few minutes passed before a tiny silhouette was seen behind plush Egyptian curtains. Jamaika stepped further up the driveway with a soft smile tugging at her lips.

"Hey, boo boo."

The screams of Jamaika's four-year-old echoed throughout the quiet neighborhood. "MOMMY!"

She bent to hug her son tightly and planted noisy kisses on his forehead. School was just about the only time her child left her sight, so she missed him when he was away.

"How was school?" Her hand fell to her son's forehead where a new scratch now resided. "Where did this come from, baby?"

"I fell at recess. It doesn't hurt though," he assured her and clutched a colorful drawing. He held it up to Jamaika in excitement. "Look what I made in art class!"

Jamaika cocked her head thoughtfully and nodded. "Ooh! It looks good, baby. We're going to hang it up on the fridge when we get home, okay?"

"Look at you, switching up your hairstyle." Her mother's fingers sifted through her dark hair.

"Just trying something new."

"It's cute!"

"Thank you." Jamaika smiled and hugged her mother. "And thanks again, for picking him up. I'll call you later, Momma."

She took the freeway home with the sweet sounds of childlike chatter as her only music. Occasionally, she would look back in the rearview and got a kick out of her bubbly passenger. Her son was named Levi, not Leviticus, and like his father, was a gorgeous shade of melanin and had charisma and wisdom beyond his years. He was an Honor Roll student and had been skipped from K-4 to K-5.

A homemade cheese and sausage pizza and soft breadsticks were made and served, homework was completed, a bath was given, and Levi was tucked under a throw blanket while a movie played in the living room. She settled in her office, just feet from her son's view, with a sigh. The day had been a long one, and besides the hair salon, this had been the longest she was relaxed and immobile. Since she made Senior Editor-in-Chief at Lisle Tribune, work was nonstop. But she was thankful for the pay raise and greater opportunity to exercise her love of journalism.

Jamaika's tummy hummed lowly and her eyes burned with fatigue. She had not eaten anything today, not that she even had an appetite. She wished she had eaten a slice of pizza with her son, because now her head was starting to hurt from lack of nourishment. Soon, she welcomed much needed sleep. Hours seemed to march on before she stirred awake at the familiar cologne that overtook her.

To her surprise, she was no longer clothed in her cream blouse and grey skirt. Jamaika glanced down at her body. She now wore a camisole and matching boy shorts. On her feet were her favorite velour socks. She smelled vanilla candles and then glanced up in confusion.

"What in the world?"

A smooth back met her sleep-filled vision. From left shoulder blade to right were the footprints of their son tattooed there. A pair of broad shoulders and muscular arms moved leisurely, flexed perfectly, and just looked downright delicious.

"Did I wake you?"

Levi had managed to change her clothing, place her in bed, undress himself and she had not felt a thing. She was glad to have her man back from a business trip and just an arm's length away. He turned then, probably wondering why he had not received an answer and his stare sent chills up and down her spine.

"No, you didn't wake me. Hey, baby."

She blew a kiss his way and watched the way he held their sleeping son in his arms. He looked in love all over again.

"Hey, you."

Jamaika scooted further up in bed, shook her head, and wished she had not been snoring upon his arrival. He stood and motioned for her to follow him into Levi's large bedroom. Various shadows danced along the light blue walls, and a soft tune played from the motion nightlight.

Jamaika watched as their son was tucked tightly in bed, kissed with the sweetest of kisses, and watched over with total adoration. She backed slowly from the room, said a final prayer over her family, and half-expected the hug from behind.

Jamaika placed her hands atop Levi's and leaned against the wall of his broad chest. They maneuvered ever so slowly from one end of the hallway to the next. She had missed being held by him and missed his simple but big affection.

"You're finally home."

He nodded with his sleepy, hooded eyes unmoving. His body danced to a leisure groove only she understood, and then he pulled her closer into him. His face settled in the crook of her neck.

"Finally."

"I thought your plane didn't touch down 'til midnight?"

He said nothing as he looked towards the clock. Jamaika's gaze followed. It was a quarter past one. He chuckled, revealing his sexy smile she loved so much.

"Your hair is beautiful. When did you get it done?"

Jamaika's eyes crinkled with her gigantic grin. He always noticed the little things, and it made him all the more special, sexier, and all the more hers.

She fingered her shorter locks gently; she was happy that he loved her new look. "Today." She moved to stand before the vanity mirror.

"Ah-uh, c'mere." Jamaika's wrist was cuffed and pulled, and her body ended up wedged between his legs. He sat her down on his lap and folded his hands atop her protruding stomach. His eyes softened immediately and focused on their newest creation in pure awe.

"The kids missed you." She pointed out softly.

She was referring to Levi and the growing baby inside of her tummy. He had declared it would be a girl, and already had a name picked out for her. Cali.

"I missed them more."

Jamaika ran a finger down his jawline in admiration. By day, Levi was a top-notch Public Relations Director for his self-made digital magazine, The Lion's Den, but right now he was just Levi. He was her one and only love, best friend and her husband. He could take off his many hats and just relax. He could be himself and love on her like he wanted. It didn't matter that she was 18 pounds heavier with swollen feet much of the time.

She was simply honored to carry his child and share this life with him.

"And I almost lost my mind not having their mother with me."

Levi rubbed at the fullness of her waistline. She was showing more since two weeks ago when he left her, and it looked good on her, along with the natural glow she always developed while expecting.

God had given them the desires of their hearts and blessed them with beautiful, healthy children. Doctors told Jamaika she would never be able to conceive, and she wished she could visit every specialist who had given her that diagnosis.

"I left you some food wrapped up on the…" Her words were silenced by a set of soft fingertips. Jamaika smiled coyly at the brown eyes staring back at her. "Stove."

The finger was replaced by a kiss that was slow and deliciously long. "What did you make?"

Jamaika wrapped her arms around herself and watched him move out of the bedroom. He was dressed comfortably in socks, boxer-briefs, and a bare chest. This was her preferred night clothing on him.

"Your favorite."

"When we checked on the kids, did you see Levi sleeping with his butt in the air?"

"Yeah, I noticed it the other night too. I don't know where he gets it from," Jamaika giggled and leaned against the granite countertop.

"You."

"I do not do that," she protested and bumped him playfully with her hip.

"Mmm, this smells good, baby." Levi warmed up his plate and migrated back to their bedroom with his wife in tow. She settled into his side and leaned her head against his shoulder. They shared bites of the pizza slices every so often and kissed here and there.

"How did your trip go?" Jamaika wrapped her arm in his and nuzzled a cheek against his warm skin.

"Really well. There's a new rapper coming out of Washington that they want me to brand and help market. I told him I'd give him a feature in The Lion's Den. You got my text about yesterday's meeting?"

She nodded.

"Yeah, it involved our plan for the new office to open up in Los Angeles. That'll happen at the top of the year hopefully, in late January."

"I'm so proud of you."

Levi put his plate down on the floor and pulled Jamaika onto his lap. She suddenly leaned over, grabbed the remote and turned on the television. As always, recorded sports footage awaited him.

"Oh, I taped that LeBron James documentary you missed last night."

"I just want to talk to my wife and hold her right now. I'll watch that later. How was your day?"

His eyes remained on her. She was always in wife mode and as much as he appreciated her gesture, he had missed her.

Jamaika thought back to the day's events. It was the nightly routine that made up much of their marriage. At least once out of the month, she would stay up late to see him home after a business trip, and he would eat the night's dinner over TV and a little Q&A before drifting off to dreamland without her.

Once everyone was in bed and asleep, Jamaika snuck off to the balcony with her laptop and worked until early morning to begin the cycle all over again. Despite her toxic marriage to Jalen, and blinded dedication during their rocky relationship, she knew now that she was created to be Levi's helper. Jamaika didn't take their love for granted and was in it for the long haul with respect, patience, and unconditional love.

Things were silent before long as fatigue slowed his movements and speech. Levi had fallen back on the bed with her nestled against him completely. His hands rubbed at her backside and thighs. Jamaika wiggled free from her boy shorts, all the while he watched in interest and then he propped his head up to catch a better angle of her scene.

"What do you have planned for tomorrow?"

Her husband's arms reached for her. "What you say?" Levi's lips settled on her collarbone. "Mmm. You smell good."

Her fingers played with the nape of his neck as his played in her hair.

"I said, what do you have planned for tomorrow? I was thinking we could take Cree to school together…"

Her beautifully spreading hips were his focal point.

"…Come back and eat breakfast in bed, and just stay here all day until he's done at three. Are you listening?"

Levi was obviously listening but not hearing. "Uh huh, uh huh."

"I just want relaxation with no phones, no TV, no computer…just me and you. Feel me?"

He pulled his lips between his teeth sexily and his eyes lowered. "I want to feel you." A large hand cupped her ample backside to lift the satiny gold tank top upward. "C'mere."

"I thought we were talking right now?" Jamaika giggled and pulled her lingerie back down.

"Believe me, I'm done." Levi glanced up into her eyes hungrily. "You stop talking and make love to me."

"Make me." Jamaika tried standing but his strong hands weighed down on her hips. "It's been a long day and you're making demands at me?"

He exhaled heavily and yanked her further up on the bed with him. His left eye closed in a mischievous wink.

"I won't mess up your hair."

She lifted an eyebrow. "Promise?"

"You have to promise not to scream first. We can't be waking Levi up on a school night." Jamaika's mouth fell open in shock, and he covered it with his own mouth for a moment. "You realize it's been two weeks, four days, and nine hours? I need you."

With his eyes still on her, she lowered her eyelids and puckered her lips. It was a look she had mastered over the years. She could feel from where she sat, his excitement soar and mouth water. Oh, she had him. Her legs tightened around his waist and she rolled them over to blowing out candles and turning off the light. The cool sheets were thrown over their heads and they shared secret smiles as she whispered his favorite song back to him.

"Then take me."

Nearly a half hour later, Jamaika was pushing dark tresses out of her face and tugging on a bathrobe. "I love you," were their final words to one another as he rolled over and welcomed a deep sleep, heavy breathing, and all.

Jamaika tucked the covers around him, suppressing a yawn before tiptoeing upstairs with her work in hand. It would be another long, tiring night and even drowsier morning, but she had the next few days off, so it was worth it.

She decided to write her column for the newspaper early. It was not due for another week, but she decided to get a head start. As her fingers typed, and her thoughts flowed, she felt an indescribable joy overtake her. She was exhilarated. She was thankful. Levi was the perfect companion and lover to her, and she wished they had found each other sooner.

He had never raised his voice or his hands to her and was always a gentle giant. He was her biggest supporter and a great encourager. Levi was her balance when she was stressed, and her muse when she was uninspired. Oh, how he defended and protected his family, and she marveled at how wonderful he was at fathering.

Jamaika often found herself in awe at the way he held and interacted with Levi. Even the way he tended to his boo-boos or calmed his tantrums was admirable. She could not wait to see how he would be with their baby girl. He was attentive to his family, and provided, as a real man should.

She had not always done things right in life, but she would forever thank God for her beautiful, ever-growing family. She would forever praise the Creator for His favor, and her answered prayers.

"Thank You, God," she whispered up to the Heavens.

She vowed to always honor the Lord for satisfying her soul's cry.

The End

Thank you for reading! Please read Lord Save Me From Myself to continue this incredible series.

Please consider leaving a review on Amazon/Goodreads, and if you are so inclined, write to the author herself at ***info@osrbooks.com***.

Reviews and word-of-mouth recommendations mean EVERYTHING to the author.

ABOUT THE AUTHOR

Olivia Shaw-Reel has written nearly 30 books before her 30th birthday. Her award-winning novels, *Soul Cry*, *What God Has Joined Together, and Matters of the Hart: A Tale of the Dysfunctional Hart Sisters*, have become her biggest-selling books to date.

She also hosts *The Reel Love Podcast* with her husband, Paris. Olivia lives in Milwaukee, WI.

Visit the official storefront for updates and to purchase autographed paperbacks at ***osrbooks.com***.

Follow her on Instagram, Clubhouse, TikTok, Facebook and Twitter at ***@oliviashawreel***.

OTHER TITLES FROM THE AUTHOR

Soul Cry, Vol. 3
What God Has Joined Together, *2-Book Series*
Baptized in Her Seduction: A Church Love Affair,
2-Book Series
Lord, Save Me From Myself, Vol. 2
Meet Me at the Altar
Full Court Mess
The Only Gift
Andrue & Sy'mone: An Urban Love Affair, *3-Book Series*
Can't Leave Him Alone After the Love We Made,
Book 1
Kiss Me @ Midnight
Stuck Wit'chu
Sins of a Mafia Princess
Matters of the Hart: A Tale of the Dysfunctional
Hart Sisters, *3-Book Series*
In Love With Everything You Could Be
Stalked by My Pastor, *Book 1*
A Christmas Miracle
Who's Loving You This Christmas?
Saved, Sanctified, & Filled With Anxiety
Compilation